Within
Darkness

Within
Darkness

C.J.M. NAYLOR

C.J.M. Naylor
cjmnaylor@gmail.com

Cover Design by Alexander von Ness

Printed in the United States of America

First Edition

To Grandpa Roger.

Together again with Paula.

CHAPTER ONE

I repeated after the priest.

"I, Abigail Lu Jordan, take thee, Phillip Michael Hughes, as my lawful husband. To have and to hold, from this day forward, for better, for worse, for richer, for poorer, in sickness and in health, until death do us part."

Phillip looked into my eyes. His were radiant, excited. This was the day we had long been planning for. This was the day we would start the rest of our lives. Together, with our families, at St. Patrick's Cathedral.

The priest spoke. "I join you together in marriage, in the Name of the Father, and of the Son, and of the Holy Ghost. Amen."

The priest then did the blessing of the rings, and Phillip took mine. As he placed it on my finger, he said, "With this ring, I thee wed; this gold and silver I thee give; with my body I thee worship; and with all my worldly goods I thee endow."

But then Phillip withdrew the ring.

"But you let me die," he said. "You killed me, Abigail."

"You let us all die."

I turned and saw my parents before me. They were wearing the same clothes from the day they had died. And as I looked at Phillip

1

now, I realized he was wearing the same clothes too.

"Like you said," Phillip said, leaning in to whisper into my ear, "till death do us part. The problem is it already has."

"No," I said softly.

"You are a killer," a voice whispered in my ear.

I turned and saw Bessie's decaying body next to me. Her head was cocked to the side, surveying me in a vulnerable state.

And then there was darkness.

August 1944 - Six Months Later

My screams filled the entire room. I was flinging around in my bed sheets. I felt like I was drowning in them. The room was dark. I couldn't see.

"Abigail!"

I heard Bridget, but I couldn't see her. Where was she? I continued to fling my arms in desperation. I had let Phillip die. I had let my parents die. I had let them all die.

Arms entangled me, but I continued to flail.

"Calm down," Bridget spoke. "Abby, calm down."

Her voice did the trick, as it had for months now. I began to cry. The tears came quickly, and I let myself fall into Bridget's arms, and she comforted me.

"Shhh," she spoke. "It's okay. I've got you."

That only made me cry harder. It reminded me of Phillip. The way he would speak to me, the way he would hold me when something wasn't right. Why did he have to die? Why did I let him die?

Bridget laid me back on the bed after the tears had subsided. Slowly, I fell back to sleep.

The next morning, I sat out on our balcony of the Chambord Building, drinking the morning tea Ian had made for me after my rough night. The city of San Francisco was awake and lively. I could hear the everyday city traffic, the bell of the cable cars, and the voices of on-foot travelers. Bridget had already left for her classes that day, and Ian had gone to the American Headquarters. Bridget and I transferred to the University of San Francisco when we moved here six months ago. Along with my educational studies, I was supposed to be studying with the American Timekeeper. When Councilor Headrick come here with me, to help Bridget and I settle in, I told her I didn't want to see the American Timekeeper. She had become angered by the situation, but she didn't force me. She told me to contact her when I was ready. I wouldn't be ready. I also have not been going to class. I dropped out shortly after we had arrived and haven't left my apartment since. Needless to say, Bridget is concerned for me. But I think I'm fine.

I had no intentions of meeting the American Timekeeper. I wanted nothing to do with that life. As the boat that brought us to America had crossed over the ocean, the long ride brought my true feelings to the forefront. I decided I would ignore the premonitions —I wouldn't encourage the voices as I had done my whole life. I would let them fall into my subconscious. The fact that I descended from an original Timekeeper made no difference to me. I wouldn't indulge in the premonitions any longer. And I found that the more I continued to ignore them, the more they left me alone. But they had ways of getting through to me.

Dreams. The dreams I could not control. I had freedom for the first two months we had settled in. I was enjoying my classes. Now and then, Bridget and I would go out for a night on the town. I liked San Francisco, I did. It brought me peace that I had not known in London, in the war. There was no fear of waking up in the middle of the night to an air raid. There weren't signs plastered everywhere to wear your gas mask. Sure, things were rationed here too, and people still talked about the war, but it felt safe. I missed London, but I felt safe.

Until the dreams started.

Two months after we arrived, I experienced a painful re-imagining in my dream of the night Phillip died. At first, it was just a repeat of the events that had happened to me. It was me, having the premonition. Me, running to save him. Me, realizing I could not. But then, it was me watching him in the library. Me, watching the library collapse around him. It was that, over and over and over again. It frightened me. It caused me to wake up screaming. It caused Bridget to run into my room and wonder what was going on. She was used to it now, though. It had become an almost nightly ritual. Was this my punishment for trying to live a normal life? I knew it was because I was grieving, but every night? There was already the daytime, where thoughts of Phillip and my parents would plague my mind. But at night? Dreams were supposed to be peaceful. Welcoming. Not horrific.

The dream that I had had last night was a new dream altogether.

It was the first time I had dreamed about Bessie in months. But then, seeing Phillip. Seeing him asking why I let him die. That had not happened before. I know Phillip wouldn't have said that in reality, if he were still here. I knew he would never say that, not even think it. I realized that my subconscious must blame me for Phillip's death. I had to forgive myself. But I was afraid to. I wanted Phillip in my life —I needed him. But I couldn't have him. He was dead. I needed my mother and father—my mother who would talk to me about these things—my father who would comfort me and call me his Abigail Lu. Even Mrs. Baxter, who would say something comical and make it all better. But they were gone. They were all gone. It was just Bridget, Ian, and I. We had each other. For now, that was enough. But I worried about what would come.

I rested my head against the back of the chair and closed my eyes. I let the sounds of the city speak to me.

Killer.

My eyes flashed open, and it felt like ice went through my body. I turned my head back toward the open doorway to the living room. The room beyond was dark. It was a voice in my head. It had to be. But why did it sound like it had come from in there? I set the cup of tea I had been drinking down and stood up. My mind was playing tricks on me. That was all.

The darkness of the living room engulfed me as I entered it. I reached over for the light switch and flicked it. Nothing happened. Why was it so dark in here? Why was the power off? The light emanating into the room from the balcony stopped just a few feet from the door. Bridget had all the windows closed and shaded. I made my way to the kitchen to open up a window when I heard it again.

Killer.

The voice sent shivers down my spine. It was not a voice I had heard before. The voice was a voice that I would prefer not to hear. It sounded dark, sinister, and cold. This time it had come from my bedroom. Was it in my head? Or was there someone in my apartment?

I opened the drawer where we kept our cutlery and took out a long kitchen knife. The knife began to shake, and I realized how nervous my body was. Quietly, I made my way into my bedroom. Once again, darkness. I reached over and flipped the switch. Once again, nothing.

Killer.

The voice came from my bathroom this time. I made my way through the doorway and reached over to flip the switch. It still didn't work. The bathroom door slammed shut. I dropped the knife in fear and turned the knob on the door. It was locked. I unlocked the door and turned the knob. It was still locked.

Abigail.

The voice was right behind me. The temperature in the bathroom began to drop. I turned around slowly. Bessie appeared in the mirror above the sink. Her skin was half peeling from her body. She was smiling at me—a horribly evil smile. She then began to climb out of the mirror and with her came water. Water poured forth from the mirror. It was the water from the River Thames.

You killed me, Abigail, she said. *You let me go. You could have saved me.*

Everything suddenly stopped and I was myself again. I was standing in front of the mirror in the bathroom, simply looking at my reflection. But while Bessie was not in the mirror, preparing to climb out toward me, there was a note taped to it.

Killer.

It was written in my handwriting.

CHAPTER TWO

Bridget and I were sitting on her bed. She held the note in her hand, as she had while she listened to my story that afternoon.

"I think we should go see someone," Bridget said softly.

"No."

She gave me the look.

"Bridget, I'm not going to see anyone. I am perfectly capable of diagnosing myself. My parents died. My fiancé died. I let Bessie go. My subconscious blames me for Phillip's death. Naturally, I'm sleepwalking and left a note for myself."

Bridget still gave me the look.

"Abby," she said, "I'm not saying we don't know what the problem is. But there are people who can help make these dreams go away. It's not getting better if you are starting to sleepwalk."

"I know," I said, bowing my head. "I'm afraid though. It isn't something I'm interested in."

"Needing help," Bridget responded, "doesn't mean you are insane. It just means you're lost and you need a guide. But it doesn't have to be a doctor that you go and see."

I looked up at her.

"Then who?"

"Who do you think?" Bridget asked. "The Timekeepers. I think you should send a letter to your father and maybe consider going to see the American Timekeeper, for once. Did your father leave you an address to write to?"

I nodded. He had given it to me just before the funeral—a place where he would go and receive any written communication between him and me. I felt guilty for not writing him. I had sent him something when we had arrived, but that had been it. I supposed it had all been part of my means to escape the Timekeeping world, leaving him behind too. And I knew he didn't deserve that. Oddly enough though, he never responded.

A knock sounded at the door to Bridget's bedroom.

"That's Ian!"

"Why doesn't he just come in?" I asked. "He does live here."

"Because he's a gentleman," Bridget responded. "He was waiting for me to get dressed, of course."

Bridget jumped up and flattened the end of the white dress she was wearing. I had almost forgotten about Ian; I could talk to him about these things too. But he and Bridget were going out tonight, so it would have to wait. The two of them had recently begun dating. I had been thrilled when Bridget told me. She needed someone like that in her life, but she hadn't seemed particularly excited about it.

"Come in," Bridget announced.

The door of the bedroom opened with a little squeak, and Ian stepped in. He wore a gray button-down shirt and tie, with black slacks. He looked quite handsome indeed; dressed up and ready to take Bridget out.

"Abigail."

I had been staring out the window of my bedroom, but I turned my gaze toward Ian's voice.

"Hello, Ian," I said softly.

Ian smiled and took Bridget's hand.

"I made you a cup of tea," he said. "It's on the kitchen table."

I smiled at that. He was always thinking of me. "Thank you."

The two of them said goodnight and left the apartment, talking about where they were going. I stood there, watching them go, letting the silence envelop me.

Dear Mathias.

My eyes pored over the empty piece of paper; the tip of my pen touched the page but no words came. What could I possibly say to him after so much time had passed? Should I tell him about the dreams and the sleepwalking? I put the pen down and placed my head in my hands. Why couldn't I come up with something to say for a simple letter to my father? I picked up the pen and stopped again. I had to be careful about what I would say because of the postal censorship in the States. In the years before the war, someone talking about Timekeeping in a letter may have simply been referred to as crazy, but now they might think me an enemy of the United States. I decided to refer to Timekeeping as "family studies" and the American Timekeeper as our "American cousin."

Dear Mathias,

I have been having some nightmares lately. I keep seeing Phillip's death repeated over and over again. I can't keep it out of my thoughts during the day either. The thoughts consume me—it is terrible. Please help me.

I stared at what I had written, but I realized I could not send that to him. The last thing I wanted to do was worry him or make him feel as if I needed him then and there. I took a sip of the tea Ian had made for me, and then, without thinking any more of it, crumpled the paper and picked up a clean sheet.

Dear Mathias,

How have you been? Everything is going well in San Francisco. I have still been undecided about whether to continue my family history studies and have yet to meet with our American cousin. I understand that this is frustrating for you, but well, you'll just have to endure it.

But I want to know about you. How have you been? Are you going out? I hope that you find the courage to leave the family estate and venture out into London. There is so much life that can be sought in the city and staying cooped up in the estate will do nothing good for you. Now that you have me in your life, however far away I am, I hope that you know you have someone. You are not alone anymore.

Please write to me and tell me how you are doing. I am eager to hear from you. I wrote to you once before, when we arrived, but never received a response. Perhaps my letter was lost in the mail? It wouldn't be surprising given the state of things.

I hesitated before I decided to lie. I didn't want to sound depressed and alone by saying I had dropped out of university.

I have been busy taking classes at the University of San Francisco, as well as tending to the apartment with Bridget. I hope to hear from you soon.

Truly,

Abby

Lying is a sin.

My entire body froze. The voice, it was Bessie's voice. Slowly, I turned around, my heart pounding against my chest. But there was no one there. I was alone. Was I losing my mind this time?

I turned back to the letter and quickly folded it up and placed it inside an envelope. The letter would have to do. Sure, I fibbed a little bit, but I couldn't make him worry. He was finally getting back to enjoying life, at least I hoped. It was more than I could say for myself.

I left the letter for Ian to mail out when he went to the Headquarters, because of the fact that I did not go outside anymore, except for the balcony, ever. If there was a fire, I guess I would die, because I was no longer a part of the world outside these walls or the world of Timekeeping.

CHAPTER THREE

What happened yesterday had not left my thoughts. It was consuming me. I wondered if it was possible to be haunted by ghosts, if they even existed. I laughed at myself—of course, it was possible. Look at the world I had found myself in.

I looked at my reflection in the mirror across from my bed, where I was lying. It's my favorite place. My hair was down around my shoulders, but it stuck up in various places. There were dark patches under my eyes. It was hard to sleep, when as soon as I did, I were awarded with nightmares. It was also evident I had lost weight. I hadn't been eating as much—my appetite never having been quite the same since Phillip died.

This was the girl I had become: a lifeless corpse that continued living. It was as if I was numb in the weeks after my parent's deaths. But Phillip's death was the icing on the cake. Was this what war did to a person? Was this how every other person who had lost someone in the war felt? Would it have been better if my parents and Phillip had died naturally, and not tragically?

The door to my room creaked open, and I saw Bridget peering in through the crack. I looked at her. I'm sure the look she received said, *What the hell do you want?* She didn't deserve it. I knew that. She had lost her father in the war. She knew the feeling. And on top of that, she had been left living with her stepmother—a woman who had never wanted her.

Upon seeing that I was awake, she pushed the door open and walked in. Ian followed behind her.

"You should be getting out of bed, Abby."

I shot daggers at Bridget. "I haven't been up for long; it's still early."

That was a lie. I had no idea what time it was, and I had been staring at the mirror for quite some time.

"Abby, it's three o'clock in the afternoon."

I laughed out loud. It wasn't at them. It was at me. Of course, it was three in the afternoon. I was letting my life fade away, but what did it matter? Seriously, what did it matter?

"We've made an appointment for you," Bridget blurted out, "to see someone."

This time I did laugh at her. Of course, she had made an appointment with someone. Phillip wasn't around to argue with her this time. She could take matters into her own hands. It was very Bridget.

"You can cancel."

I didn't look at her as I said it. I continued to be drawn to my reflection in the mirror.

"We're not going to. You're not well, Abby," Bridget said. "You need to see someone. You are going to see this doctor whether you like it or not."

I was livid. I knew that my expression contained that. I looked to

Ian for support, but he just stood there stoically.

"You will have to drag me out of this bed," I spat, "if you want me to go to this doctor."

They weren't going to control my life. I was in charge, no matter what anyone said.

"That won't be necessary."

The accent was American. I looked at the doorway and saw a man, probably in his late fifties, standing in the doorframe. He wore a tweed jacket, and was quite thin. His expression was somber, but at the same time, it was as if he was angry with me. And he didn't even know me.

"You've got to be joking," I said.

"Miss Ward," the man said, "and Mr. Cross, I'll take it from here."

Bridget nodded, and Ian took her hand. They walked out of the room together, but before she shut the door, Bridget looked at me, and I could tell she cared.

"I'm sorry, Abigail."

I heard Ian tell her not to apologize for helping and he shut the door himself. Rather angrily, I might add. Why was he so upset?

Grudgingly, I looked over at the man I assumed to be a doctor. He pulled the chair that was next to my wardrobe directly in the front of the bed and sat down. He didn't even ask if he could. I suppose when someone was emotionally distraught, manners went out the window. He focused his attention on me.

"It is a pleasure to meet you, Abigail."

"I would say the same," I responded, "but given the

circumstances of our first acquaintance, I'm not sure I can reciprocate the feeling."

He either chose not to respond to my curtness or didn't care. He cleared his throat and continued.

"Miss Ward and Mr. Cross have enlightened me of your current situation," he said. "I will tell you, that from here on out, everything we discuss in here is confidential to only the two of us. And if you truly do not want me to return after today, I won't. I cannot force you to do something that you do not wish to do. You are an adult, and you are free to make your own decisions. My name is Dr. Aldridge. I am a retired psychologist from the San Francisco area, and I specialize in treating patients who have suffered severe trauma. Abigail, tell me, do you want to spend the rest of your life in this state? Do you think Phillip would want that? Do you think your parents would want that?"

My eyes shot daggers at him. Who did this guy think he was? Wasn't I supposed to be telling him my problems?

"Of course, they wouldn't," I spat, "but they aren't here. That's the problem. They can't tell me what they would and would not want."

"Do you blame yourself for their deaths?"

"Yes."

"But it wasn't your fault," he went on. "It was a result of the war, of being in the wrong place at the wrong time."

He had no idea. I couldn't fathom how Bridget and Ian felt that this was helping the situation. This man did not know the world of Timekeeping and the fact that it was my fault. I had seen Phillip's death, and I had let him die. Mathias had seen the deaths of my parents, and he had let them die. We saw death as it would happen and there was not a damn thing that we could do about it. He had no idea. There was no way he could.

"It's more complicated than that," I said.

"How so?"

How could I tell him without telling him? I remembered the night my parents died. I had run back into the house to help them, but maybe if I hadn't done that, they would still be here. I repeated the story of what happened that night to him. How my mother had urged me to stay in the shelter. How I had deliberately ignored her requests and went for her. Maybe, she would have survived somehow if I had chosen differently? Maybe, if I had stayed in the shelter, things would have gone differently? I could hear the sirens. Their sounds were piercing my eardrums. The bombs were dropping. The house was collapsing around me. I closed my eyes because tears were starting to come. I felt a hand on my shoulder, and I opened my eyes. The tears poured out and wet my cheeks.

"You cannot reflect on what you could have done differently," Dr. Aldridge said. "If you do, then you will always blame yourself."

Dr. Aldridge gave me a business card that detailed his location in the city and how he could be contacted. He urged me to contact him again for another appointment. I told him I had no idea how I was going to pay him. I wasn't working. Bridget was, and Ian was, but it barely supported us. The apartment was being paid for by Mathias—I had no idea how. He told me not to worry. He owed the world some favors he had said, and I could be one of them.

After he left, I sat and contemplated if it was a good idea. Of course, it was a good idea. But I had no idea how to continue living. I had Bridget and Ian—but my parents and Phillip—they were gone. How do you keep going after that?

"How'd it go?"

Bridget and I were both sitting at the table, sipping our cups of tea. Ian had made us both a cup before leaving for the American Headquarters. I looked up at her as I sipped my tea and simply shrugged. She sighed that annoying sigh.

"Can you elaborate?" she asked.

"I guess it went well," I said.

"Did it help to talk about your experiences?"

I laughed. "My experiences?"

"I mean what happened to you."

"Well, I'm sorry, but I can't give him all of the details about Timekeeping, and as for my own personal life, it seems you've already filled him in."

Revealing the world of Timekeeping to an outsider was, as Mathias put it, strictly forbidden. I had already pushed the envelope by telling Bridget. But how could you keep something like that from your closest friend? While Bridget knew everything, the Council—upon our arrival to San Francisco— had expressly forbidden her from entering the American Headquarters. I suppose they hadn't appreciated Mathias letting her into the London Headquarters before we left. They also weren't happy about the fact that we had to travel by boat, rather than by the Time Line, because Bridget was with us.

But that was beside the point now.

I knew Bridget well. She only wanted to know what was going on. She didn't want to involve herself. I think that was one of the things that bothered me about her. She was accepting of who you were as a person, but when it came to talking about it, she didn't offer much feedback. She almost pretended it wasn't a part of her world.

"Well, maybe there is someone else you could talk to?"

I looked at her. "The American Timekeeper? No."

"I mean, it could help," Bridget pressed, "since he would know everything."

"Or we could both go on pretending it doesn't exist."

Bridget gave me her look of annoyance again.

"Oh, don't give me that look," I spat. "You know as well as I do that you aren't interested in what doesn't involve Bridget. If it doesn't pertain to you, you'd rather not hear about it."

She shot me a look that said I had gone too far. Without saying anything, she removed herself from the conversation, as always. I sat at the table, sipping my tea by myself. Even after Mathias had let her into the London Headquarters, she was still a skeptic, and not only about Timekeeping. Before Bridget's father had died, she informed him she no longer wished to go to church. She told him she had conflicting beliefs. At the time, she still believed in God. But now, I wasn't so sure she believed in God anymore.

Her father had blown up at her, and they fought. After that, he was drafted, and he was killed in the line of duty. Bridget's last memory of him had been fighting with him the night before he had deployed. I think her father's death pretty much sealed her beliefs, but she never said otherwise.

I'm not a saint though. I haven't been to church since Phillip's funeral because I have no idea why God would allow such terrible things to happen. Why would he create someone who had to endure something as tempting as seeing when a person would die but not be able to do anything about it? The only thing they were allowed to do was view the horrible things people in the world did to each other, the horrible things they would do, and not be able to do a thing to stop it. I had no idea what to think. At least my father could have sacrificed himself if he prevented someone's death, but I couldn't even do that. Because I was an original Timekeeper, I was subjected to a harsher a fate—a fate that would destroy the world, as we knew it.

Drip.

The room suddenly became cold, sending a shiver down my spine.

Drip. Drip. Drip.

What was that sound? And then a horrible, rotting smell found its way into my nostrils and I had to place the tea down and cover my nose. The smell was so overbearing. I had never smelt death before, but that is what it smelt like. And then on my shoulder, I felt a hand. A cold, wet hand. My heart began to beat faster, and I began to take deep breaths as I slowly turned my neck to see who was behind me. And then I was looking into the eyes of Bessie, her eyes sunken and hollow, her skin peeling away from her body. She was soaked to the bone from the water of the Thames.

You're a killer.

I let out a scream and threw myself to the floor, scrambling away from her as quickly as I could.

"Abby?" I heard Bridget call.

Bessie began to move forward, a puddle of water beneath her as she walked closer and closer and closer.

"Get away from me!"

And then Bridget's hand touched my shoulder and everything disappeared.

"Abby? Are you okay? What's wrong?"

I didn't respond. I simply let myself go limp in Bridget's arms as darkness fell upon me.

Bessie's hand clung to mine. I was in charge of whether she lived or fell to the watery depths of the Thames. How can you decide to let someone live that has destroyed so many lives? This woman had murdered my mother, and for what, I still didn't know. If I let her go, then I would never know. I would never know the truth about what happened that day. But how could I know the truth? This woman had lied to me from the beginning. She had let me believe that Mathias was a terrible person, a person capable of killing his wife. Ian was there as well, telling me not to trust her; telling me to let her go.

I had let go of her arm, and she had fallen, her scream piercing the iciness of the night, to the river below. The water that she had used her strange powers on was electric. It electrocuted her entire body, peeling the skin away from her. The horrific sight haunted me.

Once again, I woke up from my deep, nightmarish sleep, gasping for

21

air. Bessie's peeling flesh was glued to the forefront of my mind. She was falling. I had let her go. I didn't save her. I had killed her. I was a killer. I had killed Phillip. I had killed my parents. I was a monster that needed to be put down.

I remembered something I had never processed before. Ian had told me to let her go, and Bessie had looked as if she was betrayed. It was like she knew him, but did she? I had forgotten these facts after that day, and especially after Phillip had died. They had left my mind. They were more secrets that needed to be answered. But I didn't want to be a part of this world. I wouldn't seek out the American Timekeeper. I needed to know more from Mathias; he was my only source.

CHAPTER FOUR

September 1944

Several weeks had passed, and there had been no response from Mathias. I had no idea how the international post worked, especially during the war, but there was no way it should take this long. Perhaps someone had censored it and thought it too suspicious? I doubted that. It must have gotten lost in the post. I decided to try and write another letter. Once again, as I put pen to paper, I had to be discreet and refer to Timekeeping as something else.

Dear Mathias,

Perhaps you didn't receive my last letter? Or maybe it hasn't arrived yet. But either way, I needed to write this because of some memories that I have been thinking about, of the night that Bessie died. I guess I just need to get some of these thoughts off of my chest. I keep reliving that night, over and over, in my dreams. I sometimes wonder if I will ever truly be rid of it.

I was also wondering if you could tell me more about my mother, Elisabeth. How did you two meet? It would give me some more comfort to know more about her. Even after everything, I found out several months ago, I still feel like we are separated by time, and that I know very little of her.

I hope to hear from you soon. I miss you! San Francisco is wonderful! I went out with Bridget and Ian the other night for a night on the town. It was great to take a break from our studies.

Yours,

Abigail

I didn't like lying. But I didn't want him to worry. He didn't deserve that after everything he had been through. This was how I convinced myself that my lies were okay. I couldn't focus on the fact that I was deceiving him. It was for his own good.

Is it? Or are you just a terrible person? Remember you have killed.

This was my voice. The voice that had always talked to me, had always been mine. But this time, it was dark and cold. Instead of it asking who I trusted, it insinuated that I was responsible for all of these terrible things. It made me want to crawl into a hole. Was I finally losing it?

You are a killer!

I put my head on the table and covered my ears. But of course, that didn't do anything.

Killer... killer...

The words were frantic. Over and over and over again, they poured into my head. I couldn't stop them. I needed to stop them. This was madness! I couldn't take the madness! I felt like I was going insane. I suddenly jerked myself up from the chair and it hit the floor.

"Shut up!" I yelled. "Shut up!"

I started grabbing things and throwing them. I had an empty cup on the table that I picked up and threw against the kitchen wall. It shattered into a thousand pieces. I picked up the pen that I had been writing with and threw it.

I was screaming at the top of my lungs, and I dropped to my knees and put my head into my hands. Telling the voices to shut up didn't do much. They continued...

Killer... killer...

Through the word "killer" being repeated constantly and my screaming, I could vaguely hear footsteps. My vision was blurring because of the tears pouring from my eyes. My mouth was salivating because I was crying and screaming at the same time. I was shaking. I felt hands on my shoulders, and I think someone was screaming at me. But I had no idea what was going on anymore. All I heard were the words, over and over and over again. They wouldn't leave me alone. Between the voices, my screams, and my cries, I think I must have gone numb. I heard another voice, a man's voice. Ian, maybe? But I didn't know anymore. It was them and me. Me and them. Me.

Them. Them. Me. I didn't know; I didn't feel, them and me. Me, them, me, them. Ouch. Something pinched me. And then it was just —

Killer... killer...

Sunlight was creeping in through my bedroom window. It seeped under my eyelids, and while I didn't want to, I peeled them open. I was in my room in the comfort of my bed. I looked down at myself and saw that I was in my nightgown. I had a terrible headache, and my face hurt. I lifted a finger to touch my cheeks and immediately withdrew it. Upon touching my cheek, there was a horrible, piercing pain.

The door to the room creaked open, and Bridget peered in. Upon seeing that I was awake, she turned to someone behind her and whispered something. The door opened wide, and Bridget came into the room, followed by Dr. Aldridge. Bridget sat at the foot of my bed, and Aldridge sat in the same chair as he had a few weeks ago.

"I was hoping you would make an appointment to see me," he said. "We might have been able to avoid some things."

"What happened?"

I looked at Bridget and saw she was starting to cry.

"Abby," she whispered. She took a brief moment and then started to explain. "You went into some sort of fit. I came out of my room, and you were in the living room screaming. You were on your knees. Your hands were covering your ears. You kept screaming, and crying, and shouting. You were saying, 'Shut up! Shut up!' over and over again. You...you even ripped out some of your hair."

Dr. Aldridge stepped forward. "Abigail, Bridget contacted me, and I came as quickly as I could. When I got here, you were still in the same fit. Because you were not in your right mind to make decisions regarding your own health, I quickly administered a sedative. One injection of amobarbital and you were sleeping like a baby. You've been going in and out of consciousness for the last twenty-four hours."

"You drugged me?" I gave them both a look of shock. I couldn't decide if I was angry with them or angry with myself. I never thought that I would need to be... to be... sedated. I felt ashamed of myself. Why was this happening?

"I'm sorry, Abigail," Aldridge said. "It was in your best interest. I didn't want you to hurt yourself any more than you already had."

I nodded and looked down at my hands. My hands had ripped out my hair while trying to stop the voices; because the voices were mine. Yes, I could hear voices because I was a Timekeeper, but this was something else entirely. It was the voice that had been speaking to me directly, since my eighteenth birthday. But it was different too. It had been accusatory.

"Abigail, have you ever heard of combat stress reaction?"

My eyes drew away from the weapons—my hands. I looked at Dr. Aldridge confused. Why was he talking about combat?

"Combat stress reaction, or sometimes called shell shock," he began, "is an illness that we have been treating soldiers for. After suffering traumatic conditions, they tend to have nightmares, maybe visions, hallucinations, panic attacks, you name it. While the term shell shock was used for soldiers who were involved in explosions of some sort during World War One, there is a link between the trauma that you have suffered and what is happening to you now. You were in the house that collapsed on you and your parents. You saw your father's body. You saw your mother's body. And then, only a week later, your fiancé—"

"Stop," I say firmly. "I don't need you to repeat what happened to me. I know what happened. I was there. I'd rather not have the images painted in my mind again today. Are you trying to say that I have shell shock…or this combat stress reaction?"

"Yes," Aldridge said. "And I'd like to propose that you come and stay somewhere else so that we can guarantee your safety."

Bridget looked at him, shocked. Apparently, this had not been in the discussions they had been having.

"Doctor," Bridget said politely, "do you think that is necessary? I mean she is perfectly capable of staying here. I'm here, and so is Ian."

"Miss Ward," Aldridge said, "I understand your concern. But my ultimate concern is for the safety of Abigail, and the safety of you and Mr. Cross. If you had not been here yesterday, I fear the worst could have happened. And even if you had been here, if you had not been quick to call me, well, anything can happen when a person is not able to comprehend the difference between hallucination and reality."

"Are you going to force me?"

Aldridge smiled a smile that seemed poisonous to me. I don't know why. I liked him—I think. But there was something off about him that I couldn't put my finger on.

"I can only force you," he said, "if you are deemed as a danger to yourself and society. I cannot make that decision on the evidence of one incident. But if you did come to the point of being dangerous, then you could be involuntarily committed."

"She's not dangerous!" Bridget looked at the doctor with wild eyes.

"I'm sorry," Dr. Aldridge said. "I'm not trying to upset either of you. I only want what is best for Abigail. The hospital I work out of, St. Ignatius's, is located here in San Francisco. We would be able to house Abigail there and monitor her until she gets better. But it is your decision, Abigail. But I would strongly recommend that you choose it."

"I think it would be a good decision."

I looked up at Ian. He was standing in the doorway. He had come out of nowhere.

Bridget looked at him. "Ian!"

I could tell Bridget was changing sides now—how convenient. She only wanted me to see someone, but lock me up and throw away the key? How dare they?

Ian walked over to Bridget and pulled her into his arms. She was visibly shaking now. He held her and rubbed her lower back.

"I only want what's best for her," he said softly. He then looked at me. There was something in his eyes that...

"Ahem."

Dr. Aldridge had cleared his throat. I assumed this was an awkward moment for him. Bridget and Ian were embracing, and I was sitting here as confused as ever.

"No," Bridget said, pulling away from Ian. "She will stay here. We can work through this together."

Dr. Aldridge appeared annoyed.

"Um," I said, "I thought this was still my decision?"

Bridget looked at me, shocked. Dr. Aldridge and Ian's faces lifted a bit.

"Of course," Aldridge said. "It is your decision entirely."

"Right," I said, "well I mean it's still no, but I just wanted to make a point."

Aldridge looked annoyed again and excused himself. He spoke briefly with Bridget and Ian out in the hall. Why couldn't he speak to me? It was my decision. Maybe it wasn't anymore? Maybe he was telling them to record all dangerous activity I did from here on out? Any further evidence and he could easily have me involuntarily committed. I mean, I could hurt people after all. I laid back on my pillow and stared angrily up at the ceiling.

It was hours later. My room was dark, but there was moonlight coming in through the window. I hadn't slept. It amazed me how you could lie in one spot and contemplate everything, and how time would pass. Time didn't stop to allow you to think things over. Either you made good use of the time you had, or you let it go to waste. I didn't think I was wasting it though. Sometimes, you just needed to lie in your bed and think about the world, right?

The familiar creaking sound signaled to me that someone was coming in. "Abby?" I heard Bridget calling into the darkness. "Are you awake?"

I thought about ignoring her, but I needed someone right now. "Yes."

She entered my room and closed the door behind her. I was still staring up at the ceiling. She came around to the other side of my bed and lifted back the covers, crawling in next to me. I gave in and turned over onto my side so that we were both facing each other.

"Hi," she said.

I smiled. "Hi."

"Do you think our relationship is poisonous?"

I raised my eyebrows at this question and thought about it. The past year, and maybe even longer than that, it was constant arguing between Bridget and I. When we had grown up as children, we had never argued. We had always gotten along. But after I had met Phillip, that changed for some reason. And then after that, it was over and over and over again.

"I don't know," I said. I really didn't. "I think we've argued too much, and that we are both equally guilty."

"I agree," Bridget responded. "It's hard for me to agree but I do. I have this problem with myself. I think that everything I do and say is the right thing, and that other people are simply wrong."

"Really?" I laughed. "I never noticed."

She smiled at the sarcasm.

"I think I have a problem trusting the wrong people," I said.

"What do you mean?"

"I trusted Bessie," I said. "I trusted her instead of trusting you. I just needed answers and I let myself believe everything she said. I didn't trust Mathias. I didn't trust you. But in the end, who was the manipulator? It was her—always her. And now she haunts me. I'm sorry I didn't trust you. You have no idea how sorry I am after everything else that has happened."

"I do," she said. "And I'm sorry for everything I did to you. Everything I said to you. You've been through so much, and I feel like I wasn't there for you. I should have been there for you."

"Thank you." I whispered it softly, and she scooted closer to me and pulled me into her arms. We held each other for a long time.

"Do you think I'm insane?" I whispered into her ear. "I did throw a dish at you once—unintentionally that is."

She pulled away and looked at me.

"You are not insane," she said. "You are grieving. And you will probably be grieving for the rest of your life. And there is nothing, absolutely *nothing*, wrong with that. And as far as I'm concerned, you are going to stay right here with me."

I smiled, and we continued to talk. We talked about the war, about her relationship with Ian, about Timekeeping. We just talked. And for a while, I was okay.

The water from the shower cascaded over my body, and I wanted to stay, but didn't. Today, I was going to leave the apartment. It was going to be hard, and I didn't want to. I really, really, really didn't want to. But I was going to. I owed that to Bridget. We had both opened up to each other the night before in a way that we haven't in a long time. I was going to go out into the world today.

I looked at myself in the mirror. The dress I wore was simple, white. It fell to just below my knees. I had a pair of black heels on, and my hair was pulled up into a bun. Small strands of it fell around my face. I put some powder on my face and a little red lipstick. And as my mother had taught me, I pinched my cheeks to get some red into them. I closed my eyes and took a deep breath. And then I left my bedroom.

Bridget was at the table reading the newspaper and sipping on coffee. Ian was making eggs on the stove, and when I entered the room, he looked up, taken aback. Bridget looked up from the paper at Ian's reaction and then saw me. She smiled.

"You look lovely!"

I smiled and probably blushed. "Thank you."

"I'm sorry?" Ian said, sounding confused. "Did I miss something? Are you going out?"

I smiled at him. "Yes."

Bridget stood up and walked over to me and began prepping me for the world as a mother would. She tucked a strand of hair behind my ear and smiled at me. "You'll do great," she said.

"Bridget," Ian said, "do you think this is a good idea?"

Bridget looked up at him aghast. "What are you talking about Ian?" She laughed at him as she said it but then added more seriously, "Why wouldn't it be a good idea?"

"I mean, sweetheart," he said to her, "she hasn't been out there since we arrived here. She's been in her room since day one. She hasn't even gone to the bloody mailbox to mail her letters."

"Well," Bridget said, "I'm taking the day to go with her. And I'm not her caretaker Ian; she can manage herself just fine."

He pulled Bridget by the shoulder over to the side and started berating her quietly.

"Excuse me?" I said softly. He continued to chastise her until I spoke up. "Ian!"

He stopped talking to Bridget and looked up at me. He looked all puffy as if he was out of breath. What was his problempredicament? I didn't understand why he was acting this way.

"If you have a problem with something I am doing you can politely bring it to my attention," I told him. "As Bridget stated, she is not my caretaker. It isn't necessary to speak as if I'm not standing directly in front of you."

"My problem," Ian said, trying to remain calm, "is your health and well-being. Abby, I don't want something to happen to you out there. You aren't stable."

"Well thanks for the concern," I said, "but I'll manage just fine."

"Goddammit!" Ian's cursing reverberated off the walls of the apartment, and he grabbed his jacket and left. The door slammed shut violently behind him. A picture on the wall fell off its hook and to the floor from the vibration of the walls.

Bridget and I looked at each other. I worried she would get upset, but she just looked confused.

"I'm not sure he should go out there," I said to her, "he doesn't seem stable."

We both started laughing, and I was ready to take on the day. I would leave Ian's problems in the back of my mind.

CHAPTER FIVE

Bridget and I had lunch at Tadich Grill, an older seafood restaurant in the San Francisco area. As I sipped my water, we silently waited for our orders to arrive. We had left the apartment and come straight here, and after my little joke about Ian, we hadn't talked much. I didn't know what to think about his outburst—it wasn't like him. He was off lately, and I was concerned about him. He used to be nicer, but over the last six months, he had started to change. It was like he was growing tired of something, but of what, I didn't know. I honestly did not know much about him. From what he'd told us, his parents were dead. He had studied with Mathias, but other than that, his life was shrouded in mystery.

"I'm sorry about Ian." I looked up from my water, my thoughts disappearing at Bridget's words.

"There's no reason to be sorry," I said. "Ian isn't your responsibility."

"I know." She was biting her lip. She was nervous. She wasn't the type to be nervous. "It's just, I feel like he is trying to protect me from being hurt again. And because he's saying these things for that reason, I guess I feel responsible."

"Don't be," I said. "And I can understand why he wants to

protect you. If you two are going to be in a relationship, he should protect you, and you should protect him."

Bridget looked especially nervous now. She looked as if she was fighting something internally. Her hands were placed in front of her on the table and she was rubbing them together.

"Abby... there is something I need to tell you," Bridget said. "But I can't yet. I'm not ready."

"Then why tell me that?" I giggled at her. "Now I'm going to want to know." I took another sip of my water and then looked at her. She was more nervous and slightly agitated. Something was bothering her—really bothering her. "Bridget, you can tell me anything."

"I know," she said. "I just wanted you to know, but I'm not ready yet. I'll let you know when I am."

"I won't force you. Tell me when you're ready. But don't let it eat you up."

"I feel like a hypocrite. You didn't tell me things, and I was upset, and now I won't tell you anything, and you're fine with it."

I put my hand over hers, and something came into her eyes. She looked briefly shocked and looked up at me, but then looked away. "Don't worry," I said. "Tell me when you're ready. And we are different people. We do different things. There was nothing wrong with you wanting to know, and I should have told you. You're fine."

She gave me a hesitant smile, and we waited in silence for our food.

After lunch, Bridget and I decided to spend some time shopping around town. I could feel myself wanting to return to the safe confines of the apartment, but I pushed myself to want to stay out and continue our shopping trip. We were currently spending some time in a dress shop and I found myself enthralled in the various gowns that were lined up along the back wall of the shop.

I walked alongside the dresses and let my hand touch the soft fabric. I stopped at one dress in particular; it was black taffeta.

"If you like it," Bridget said, coming up behind me, "I could buy it for you. Maybe we could go out to one of the clubs in town some time and you could wear it."

The thought of buying a new dress and wearing it around town sounded wonderful. I let myself imagine the luxury of forgetting about all my problems, and all the pain that had surrounded me lately, and simply allowing myself to be happy.

"Maybe," I told her.

"No maybe," Bridget suddenly said. She pulled the dress off the rack and announced that I was trying it on. I let her pull me back to the dressing rooms, wondering what I had gotten myself into.

It was well after midnight, and I was sitting in front of my vanity mirror, running a brush through my hair. I remembered when I was a little girl, and my mother used to brush my hair. She loved doing it—I could tell. And I loved it when she did. There was something about it that was peaceful, I suppose. But she was gone now. It was just me.

"It's starting to happen more often."

I stopped brushing and looked up. It was Ian's voice. I hadn't realized he was still awake.

"She had an episode the other day," he said. "Aldridge came by. No, I tried. She refused."

My breath became shallow when I realized he was talking about me. It couldn't be to Bridget. I set the brush down and tiptoed across my room and opened the door to the hallway. I peered out and saw Ian down the hall, on the telephone.

"I realize you know what's best," Ian said, "but I can't exactly speed things along on my end. If she's not a danger to herself or others, then—" He stopped speaking, most likely having been cut off by the person he was speaking to.

"Yes," he said. "Yes, okay."

He hung up the phone, and I took my chance and stepped into the hallway. When the floor squeaked, he turned around and saw me.

"Who were you talking to?" I asked him.

"Mathias."

Mathias. He had been talking to Mathias. Why didn't Mathias want to speak with me? He hadn't responded to any of my letters.

"I'm sorry," Ian said. "I would have let you speak to him, but I thought you were asleep. It is morning on his end, after all. He wanted to call and check up on you. I told him you'd been writing to him, but I think he hasn't been getting the letters. It must be something to do with overseas mail right now."

"Oh," I said. "Well, what were you talking about other than that? I heard you say Aldridge's name. Does Mathias know him? And how did you know the number to get into contact with Mathias?"

Ian looked like he didn't want to say. After a moment though, he took a deep breath and spoke. "He thinks maybe you should follow

Aldridge's advice and go to the hospital. But—only until—only until you get better." Ian walked toward me and placed his hands on my arms. "We only want what's best for you Abby. I know I was little over-the-top today, but you hadn't been out of the apartment in months. And while it's great that you did get out, I was worried something would have happened to you. And as for the number, he actually called us and I forgot to ask. I'm sorry."

I stepped out of Ian's grip.

"Mathias has been wrong before," I said to him. "I'm fine. I am."

Ian smiled at me. "Okay," he said. "I believe you."

I stepped away and walked back to my room, closing the door behind me. Ian hadn't been talking to Mathias. You didn't allow someone like Mathias to call you, not get his phone number, and not tell his daughter that he was on the phone so that she could talk to him as well. Something strange was going on, and I needed to figure it out.

The Tower Bridge loomed in the distance. Phillip's hand was entwined in mine as we made our way toward it—the moonlight shining on our skin. The Thames was calm tonight—not a single patch of rough water in sight. As we reached the bridge, Phillip led me up to the walkway, and we paused about halfway down it to look out over the railing of the bridge.

"It's beautiful," I said.

"What is?" Phillip asked.

"London," I responded. "The river, Big Ben, everything. It's all beautiful."

"You're beautiful," Phillip. "You're my kind of beautiful."

He lightly touched my cheek and leaned into me—our lips touched. It wasn't a passionate kiss. It was just a kiss between two people that loved each other—a quick, meaningful gesture.

"It's time for you to go," Phillip said.

"What?"

"It's time for me to die again."

I shook my head at him. I didn't understand. He extended his arm and pointed out over the water. I turned my head and saw the aircrafts coming into the city—the bombs falling from beneath them.

"Why did you let me die? Why, Abby?"

Suddenly, the bridge began to deteriorate around me, and it took Phillip with it and then—then there was only darkness.

"Abby, Abby, wake up!"

My eyes opened, and Bridget was leaning over me. The morning sun was pouring in through the window and concern was in Bridget's eyes. She was already ready for the day—she must have heard me as she was getting ready to leave.

"Was I screaming again?" I asked her.

"No," she said, "but I did hear you groaning, and I came in here, and you were flailing around, and I figured you'd probably want out of whatever you were in."

I nodded. She was right. I never wanted to be stuck in my nightmares, but I needed sleep all the same. And the nightmares didn't seem to be going away anytime soon. For a person that never left the apartment very often, I felt exhausted.

Bridget sat on the edge of the bed and took her hand in mine. "You know what I want you to do?" she asked. "I want you to spend

41

the day preparing to go out tonight. You can wear that dress we bought you yesterday, you can get your hair done, whatever you want to do. Ian is taking me to the Verdi Club—it's a swing dancing club— and I want you to come."

"Bridget," I hesitated, "that's a little different than going to lunch. I'm sure it'll be crowded and, well, I don't know."

"It'll do you good," she responded. "Please? For me?"

"For you," I said.

She smiled and stood up. "I need to get going, but you be ready at seven o'clock." Before she left the room, she turned around again, as if she wanted to say one more thing. But she just smiled and gave a little wave before she turned and left.

The Verdi Club was one of the "in" clubs at the moment for swing dancing. Bridget and Ian came quite often, but this was my first outing. The music was wonderful, the crowd was made up of well-dressed individuals out for a good time, and there was dancing. On top of all that, the dress that Bridget had purchased for me matched the attire of everyone else. But even with all of this, I just couldn't get into any of it, and thus, I sat in the corner sulking. At least I was out and about—I hoped that would satisfy Bridget. It probably wouldn't though because as soon as we had arrived, I had staked my claim at a table and turned my attention watching her dance with Ian.

"Would you like to dance?"

I looked up to see a tall man, probably a couple of years older than I was, standing before me. He had broad shoulders, and his black suit fit well to his muscular upper frame. His hair was a sandy blond; his eyes a deep hazel, but it was his cheeky grin that really got to me. I didn't like the message it was sending, but at the same time, it sent a thrill through my veins that I hadn't felt in quite some time.

Phillip.

I quickly shook my head at the man.

"No thank you."

I turned my attention back to watching Bridget and Ian dancing together. The song was a slow one right now so the two of them were up against each other, barely an inch between them. He had his arm wrapped around her waist, and she was resting her hand in the crook of his neck as they danced in tune to the song.

"Are you sure?"

The man was still there? I turned my gaze up again, and sure enough, he stood before me. The answer was yes, I wouldn't mind dancing with him. He was handsome, and he seemed confident. But I didn't want to dance. I didn't want to be here. I wanted to be far away from here, because what I was feeling when I looked at this man made me grieve for Phillip and long for the hideaway of my bedroom.

"I said no." I didn't mean to be rude, but if that's what it took to be left alone, then it was fine by me.

"Just one dance."

Was he serious?

"No." I looked him square in the eye. But when I did, I couldn't stop Phillip from consuming my thoughts. As he always had, he came back to me so quickly. His cheeky smile, his blue eyes, and unkempt hair. I stood and pushed through the crowd of dancing people. The only goal right now was to get out of this nightclub before I started crying. A hand touched my shoulder and I around. I thought it was going to be Ian or Bridget, but it was the man again.

"Where are you going?"

Who was this man? I had never any feelings like this since Phillip. They reminded me so much of Phillip it hurt my insides.

"I can't be here right now," I said. "Let me go." He still had his hand on my shoulder and quickly dropped it. He was standing more in the light now, and I could see his features, his strong cheekbones, tan complexion, and sandy blond hair combed back for the night. There was that thrill going through me again. I turned away though.

"What's your name?" I heard him say behind me.

"None of your business," I responded.

"Will you dance with me? Just one dance?" he asked.

Seriously? I looked around the room—where was the door? I knew where the door was, of course, but this man was distracting me.

I took a deep breath and then answered.

"I need to get out of here," I said. "I can't dance right now—I just need to get out of here."

He smiled, and I felt myself melt. The way he smiled produced a feeling in my heart that I had felt only one other time. What was happening? I wasn't ready to feel these things again. I knew that I should have stayed at the apartment. He extended his hand, and I took it. His hand was firm and strong on mine. It made me feel safe.

"I'll help you," he said.

A part of me felt terrified—the idea of going somewhere with a stranger was odd. But then a part of me wanted it. I wanted to fall into this man's arms and bare my soul to him. I knew that would not be appropriate though.

He led me through the throng of people and a set of doors. Finally, we were stepping outside onto Mariposa Street. It was dark, and the temperature had dropped quite a bit—fall was here. I must have shivered without realizing it because the man spoke up and offered me his jacket.

"I'm fine," I said. "Thank you, though." We stood there like that, rather awkwardly, for an extended period. He had his hands shoved deep into his pockets, and he was leaning forward just a little on the balls of his feet.

"Do you want to get a coffee with me?" he asked.

A small chuckle erupted from within me. Was this happening? Was I really talking to this person?

"I—," I hesitated, but then, "sure. I can't be gone too long though. I just, I really need to get home."

"I know a place on this street," he said. He beckoned a little way down the street. "I'll lead you."

I didn't move though. "Before I go anywhere, I want to know your name."

He grinned, and then, finally, he sighed and gave up.

"It's Thomas," he said.

And because he had answered my request, and because he was so annoyingly persistent, I followed.

After a rather long walk, we finally arrived at a small coffeehouse. The man, I still didn't know his name, opened the door for me and we entered together. We found an empty table towards the back of the coffeehouse and took our seats. A woman came by, scribbled down our orders and walked away again.

"So," he said, "you seemed rather eager to get out of there." I noticed he was fidgeting with the napkin that the silverware had been wrapped in.

"Too many people," I responded.

"Are you not very social?" he asked. "If you don't mind my asking."

"I am," I said, but then, "I mean I used to be."

"I like your accent," he said. "This might be a stupid question, but oh well. You're British right?"

"I'm from London. I lived there my entire life, until recently, with the war." I realized I probably needed a lie. Why would I come all the way here because of the war? I could have gone to the countryside. "My friend is studying at the university, and I came here with her. What about you? Have you always lived here?"

"Born and raised," he responded. "My family has had their own, um, business here and needless to say I was expected to take over for my father after he retired."

There was something about the way he had said *business* that made me feel like it had partially been a lie.

"What kind of business?" I asked.

"Insurance," he quickly said, "boring stuff."

The waitress came with our coffees and placed them on the table with a ticket and walked away. The man reached into his pocket and pulled out a billfold. He slid out a ten-dollar bill and placed it on the ticket.

"You don't have to do that," I said. "I can pay for my own."

"It's fine," he responded. "I want to. And I realize now that you still haven't told me your name. And to top it off, I never told you my full name earlier. I'm Thomas Jane."

Thomas Jane. It only took me a moment to realize why that name was familiar to me. It was because I had heard both Mathias and Ian say it at one point in time. This man was the American Timekeeper—a young Timekeeper apparently. When he had told me his name was Thomas, my mind didn't even go there. It was a common name. And Timekeeping, that was the *family business*, as he had called it. I couldn't even begin to fathom this. I had to stay away from that world. It had taken so much from me already—I couldn't let it take even more. He had no idea who I was, and I wanted to keep it that way.

"I'm sorry," I said, "but I need to go."

He looked confused and then smiled. "But you haven't even finished your coffee. And you didn't tell me your name."

"I'm sorry," I said. "I have to go."

I stood and made my way toward the door of the coffeehouse, but his voice stopped me.

"At least tell me your name," he said.

I hesitated for a moment, and then I left the coffeehouse—leaving Thomas Jane wondering, I'm sure, about what had just happened.

CHAPTER SIX

That night, as I waited for Bridget and Ian to get home, I contemplated the evening's events over and over in my head. I wanted to go and find Thomas Jane. I wanted to talk to him; he felt like someone I could talk to. Instead, I had run away. It was more than just the Timekeeping, obviously. I was afraid of being around another man. A part of me felt some sort of attraction to him, something that I couldn't quite put my finger on. It scared me, because I felt I was being unfaithful to Phillip, even though he was dead.

The door to the apartment creaked open and I heard Bridget and Ian walk in, their laughter filling the hallway.

"Abby?" Bridget called.

"I'm in here," I called back.

Bridget pushed the door to my room open and smiled at me. Her hair had fallen out of its bun and she had just removed her earrings. She looked tired, but she also looked like she had enjoyed herself.

"Am I starting to imagine things," Bridget began asking, "or did I see you leave with a tall, handsome stranger?"

"You might have seen something like that," I responded, a smile erupting onto my face.

"I knew it!"

Bridget ran over to the bed and sat down, looking at me, clearly waiting for information. I remained seated in my vanity chair and considered what I should say.

"There really isn't much to say," I said. "We just had some coffee and I left."

"But what did you talk about?"

"Well," I began, unsure of what to reveal, but then I remembered there were no secrets between us, so I told her the truth. "I thought he was just a regular guy, but it turns out he is the American Timekeeper and I didn't want him to know who I was, so I got up and said I had to leave."

"You didn't even give him your name?" Bridget asked, clearly appalled.

"Well," I responded, "I felt like he didn't need it. If I want him to know who I am, I can easily find him on my own. I just don't know, Bridget."

"Abby," she said, "talk to me."

And so I did. I told her how I had felt close to this person, like I already knew him. I told her how I wanted to fall into his arms and pour my heart and soul out to him. I told her how I panicked, because I felt like I was betraying Phillip, and I told her that that was more so the reason of why I had left and that it really wasn't about the Timekeeping.

"I understand," Bridget said, but then she clarified, "I mean sort of. I understand what it feels like to have lost someone and to be grieving, but in your case the relationship with the person was different. The only thing that I can offer is that you have to take this on your own time, on your own terms, but you also need to remember that Phillip would eventually want you to move on."

I knew that she was right because of the letter that I still had from Phillip. It was safely tucked away in a box in my closet and I had never told anyone about it. I didn't know if I ever would tell anyone about it, but Phillip had made it very clear that he wanted me to be happy. He wanted me to move on.

"Moving onto another subject," Bridget said, "I was thinking maybe you could apply for a job. There is an opening at a place that I think might interest you."

"Oh, really?"

"Yes," Bridget said. She reached into her pocket and pulled out a folded piece of newspaper and held it out to me. I unfolded it and looked over the job listings that were in front of me. Bridget pointed out a specific job with her finger—a library assistant. I looked up at her, unsure of what to say, and she smiled at me. "I thought it might help; that maybe it would ease the pain. I know it would bring back painful memories, but I also feel that it would strengthen you in a way. It would get you reacquainted with the world."

I nodded.

"Thank you," I said. "I think I will apply."

"Really?" Bridget responded hopefully, as if she thought I may have been joking or would suddenly change my mind.

"Really," I said.

The following afternoon, I made my way to the San Francisco Main

Public Library on Larkin Street. In my handbag, I carried with me all of the necessary paperwork I might need in order to fill out a job application.

As I stood in front of the large, white building, admiring the majestic lion that stood in front as well as the white columns that supported the building, I felt as if I was being drawn to the building. It felt like some force was drawing me nearer; it felt almost as if I was being called to this place. I took a deep breath to calm myself and ascended the steps toward the entrance to the building.

As soon as I stepped inside, a woman behind the front library desk greeted me. If there was ever a definition of a librarian, she fit it. Her dark hair was pulled tightly back into a bun and she wore a black dress that covered almost every inch of her body. She also wore a pair of glasses that hung on a chain around her neck.

"Can I help you?" she asked as I approached the desk.

"I was wondering if I could submit an application?" I asked. "I saw that you had a position open for an assistant of some sort."

"All potential applicants must speak with our head librarian," she responded. "If you have a moment, I can see if he has time to meet you."

"That would be great," I responded.

She nodded and walked from behind the desk, making her way to the back of the library and disappearing through a door that was marked *Library Personnel Only*.

As I waited for her to return, my mind began to drift, and eventually I was back in one of my classes at Birkbeck College . . .

* * *

September 1942

"What is Shakespeare trying to say about the theme of honor in *Much Ado About Nothing?*" Dr. Gabel asked the class.

I was seated in my first course of the day and it was also the first class of the semester. Dr. Gabel was a well-known professor of the Shakespeare Throughout History course I had enrolled in this semester. We had been required to read Shakespeare's *Much Ado About Nothing* before coming to the first class session. After he asked his first question, my hand immediately shot into the air.

Unfortunately, someone beat me to it.

"Yes, sir," Dr. Gabel said, pointing, "in the back."

"Shakespeare wants us to question appearances versus reality," the man responded. "He wants us to question whether or not what we say is honorable is actually honorable, and, of course, vice versa."

I looked back at the man that had answered the question. He looked to be about my age, maybe a bit older, with dark hair. There was something about him that made me want to get up and go speak to him at that very moment. And then he looked at me. I knew that my face turned beat red and I immediately turned back around, lowering my face into my hands, embarrassed at having been caught staring at him.

"Excellent," Dr. Gabel responded. "And what is your name, young man?"

"Phillip Hughes, sir," he said.

"Well, Mr. Hughes," Dr. Gabel continued, "it is clear that you have interpreted the play correctly. Now, everyone, I want us to break up into partners and I am going to assign each of you a specific part of the text that you will prepare an analysis for. You will then give a brief presentation of your section during our next class."

Partners. I hated the idea of partnering up on the first day of classes and not knowing anyone. I looked around the room, wondering who I could ask to be my partner, when Phillip Hughes appeared in front of me.

"Hello there," he said to me. "I was wondering if you wanted to be partners?"

"I," I hesitated and looked around, and then continued nervously, "um...sure."

"You don't sound thrilled about the idea," he continued.

"I've just never had someone come up and ask me so directly before," I responded.

"Well, I'm a direct, to the point kind of person."

"Of course, you are," I said. "Sure, let's be partners."

"*Miss?*"

I turned around and saw that the woman had returned for me. She had her hands on her hips and was standing in a somewhat stooped position, suggesting that she had been trying to get my attention for a moment or two.

"Yes," I said, "I'm sorry."

"I said that Mr. Jane will see you now," she responded. "Go through the personnel door and take a right. He is the first office at the end of the hall."

"Thank you so much," I said, but before I went on, I suddenly processed what she had said and continued, "Did you say Mr. Jane?"

"Yes," she responded. "Mr. Thomas Jane is the head librarian here."

Thomas Jane.

I couldn't even begin to fathom how a coincidence like this could happen twice in the course of twenty-four hours. I hesitated for a moment and then decided I wasn't going through with this.

"I'm sorry," I said, "but I need to go."

I turned around and headed out the front door of the library, ignoring the lady's protests as she called after me. I was at the bottom of the library steps when I was suddenly out of breath and took a seat, right there in the middle of everything. I put my face in my hands and groaned about my decision. Why was I being this way? I knew it wasn't about the Timekeeping, it really wasn't.

"It's you."

I looked up and saw Thomas Jane standing in front of me. Seeing that I was flustered, he sat down next to me.

"My assistant librarian said that you ran out of the door," he said. "I felt compelled to see why I had so easily scared someone off."

"Well," I said, "this isn't exactly *insurance,* now is it?"

He sighed. "You caught me. I don't always like to reveal everything all at once, but neither do you I gather, considering I don't even know your name."

"You do know my name though," I told him.

"What do you mean?" he asked.

"I came over to the United States from London back in February," I told him. "I was supposed to study with the American Timekeeper, but when I got here, I chose not to."

A look of realization came over his face and he nodded.

"Abigail Jordan?" he asked.

"The one and only," I said, almost laughing.

"So that's why you didn't want to tell me your name," Thomas said. "Because you were afraid that I would convince you to return to Timekeeping, or something along those lines?"

"Something along those lines," I said, still somewhat breathless.

"Can I at least offer you a job here at the library?"

I looked at him in surprise. "Wouldn't you want me to apply or something?"

"I have full say," he said, "and I have literally had no applicants, besides you. So, it's yours, if you want it."

"No Timekeeping?"

"No Timekeeping," he said, smiling.

"What about Ian Cross?" I asked. " I don't want him to know that I've met you. They'll think I have decided to come back to Timekeeping or something."

"Well," Thomas said, "the Headquarters is located beneath the city. The structure and layout is a bit different from the Headquarters in London and Ian is able to access it from another entrance. There is also an entrance here, however. As for Ian, maybe you could just tell him you found a job in *insurance*." I tried my best to stifle a laugh.

"Why are you working, though?" I asked him.

"I have my reasons," Thomas answered, "but one is obviously because the entrance is so easily accessible here at the library."

I hesitated for a moment, thinking about the decision he had given to me.

"I'll do it," I said.

"Excellent," Thomas responded. "Let's go fill out some paperwork." He stood up and held out his hand to me.

"Shall we?"

I nodded, took his hand, and stood up. As soon as I was standing, I let go of his hand and we made our way back up toward the library entrance.

An hour later, I had, for record keeping purposes, submitted an application to be an assistant at the San Francisco Public Library. I sat in Thomas' office and waited as he looked over the application and additional materials.

"Well," Thomas said, "I think everything is in order. I'm going to just go ahead and hire you, because I can."

"Just like that?" I asked.

"Just like that," he responded. "You can start today if you'd like."

I didn't have anything better to do for the rest of the day, considering how I had spent the last few months, so I agreed. He took me on a tour of the library. The design of the building fascinated me; it was almost like being back in the London Library, but it was bigger. The vaulted ceilings and tall, glass windows made me feel like I was in a story, going on an adventure. I knew that this place could serve as a distraction for me from the painful memories that I had been coping with over the last several months.

Thomas showed me the various reading rooms as well as the upper level of the library. After he had showed me around, we were both leaning on a rail looking over the level below.

"What did you think?" he asked.

"It's beautiful," I responded, continuing to gaze up at the vaulted ceilings. "It reminds me of home." I had to stop myself then and take a deep breath, or I would become overwhelmed with emotion. It reminded me so much of the London Library and of Phillip. It reminded me of the hours upon hours that we had spent there together, doing homework, talking about books, or simply just spending time with each other. It reminded me of how that would never be the case again. It reminded me that life was gone.

A hand on my shoulder pulled me out of my brief reverie.

"Are you okay?"

I looked up at Thomas, and shook away my thoughts. Looking back at my hands on the rails, I realized I was gripping them rather tightly and I quickly unclenched them.

"I'm sorry," I said. "I was just thinking about home."

"London?"

I nodded. This was all a bit much for the day and I needed to make my way out of here before I lost it completely.

"Mr. Jane," I said, "thank you so much for this opportunity. I will be here at eight o'clock tomorrow morning, as previously discussed. But if you'll excuse me now, I really need to get home and rest."

"Okay," he said. I turned to go, but he called after me. "Miss Jordan?"

I turned and looked at him. "Yes?"

"Please feel free to call me Thomas."

CHAPTER SEVEN

That evening I decided to make dinner for Bridget and Ian. I planned to tell them I had a special announcement and that we were celebrating. My special announcement would be that I had found a job working with books and hopefully that would be okay for now and help me to get my mind off of other things. I had no idea if Ian knew Thomas also worked at the San Francisco Library, so my best bet was to say I'd found a job working in books and hope they would leave it at that.

Bridget was not home from university yet, and Ian had left me in the kitchen to cook after making us tea. I looked down at the chicken marsala I was making and began to add the marsala wine and some spices. The smell of the marsala sauce engulfed my senses. My mother had taught me how to make the recipe when I was thirteen. I remembered the day she had told me we were going to cook like it was yesterday. I had just gotten home from school and was surprised to find she was there, rather than Mrs. Baxter. When I walked into the kitchen, she announced she had gotten off work early that day and we were going to make dinner together—that she was going to teach me one of her favorite recipes.

A creak in the living room disrupted my thoughts.

I walked away from the stove and into the living room. It was dark in the room, save for the light coming from the curtained window. I took a deep breath and told myself I was hearing things. The Chambord Building wasn't exactly a new building. It made sense that pipes in an old apartment building would make noises at times.

I walked back into the kitchen and found my mother at the stove, stirring the chicken marsala. She was wearing the same dress she had been wearing the day she died, and to my horror, the piece of wood that had impaled part of her body, causing her death, was there as well, blood pouring forth from the wound. She turned and looked at me as soon as I entered the kitchen.

"Abigail," she said, her tone chiding, "you are going to let the chicken burn. You shouldn't walk away in the middle of cooking. You also shouldn't have killed me."

"I, I... I didn't k-k-kill you."

She cocked her head to the side as if I had said something unintelligent.

"Why, of course you did. You joined this Timekeeping world. If you hadn't gotten involved in all of this, who is to say that *we* wouldn't be here now."

Out of nowhere, Mrs. Baxter, my father, and Phillip appeared. They all joined hands and looked at me in disgust. And then Bessie was there. Water was dripping from her body, parts of her flesh peeled away.

"Look at what you did," she said. She walked over to me, until she was mere inches from my face and pointed at my family and my fiancé. "You did this."

"No," I said, shaking my head.

"Yes," Bessie said nodding. "You killed them all."

"No," I said again, softer this time, on the edge of tears.

Bessie only nodded this time.

The sound of the apartment door opening and closing entered one ear and went out the other.

"Abby?"

I heard my name, but like the door opening and closing, I didn't quite register it. I simply continued to look at Phillip and my family, looking at me as if I was the most horrible thing they had ever seen.

"Abby!"

Bridget ran past me, literally right through Bessie, and she vanished, as did everyone else and I suddenly realized the entire kitchen was filled with smoke. Bridget grabbed the pan of burning chicken marsala and put it in the sink, turning the water on as she did. More smoke filled the room and she quickly opened up the windows, allowing the smoke to dissipate. She walked back over to me and grabbed me by the shoulders.

"What are you doing?" she asked. "Abby? Are you listening to me? You could have burned the place down. What's going on?"

"My parents," I said. "Phillip, Mrs. Baxter, Bessie. They were all here."

Bridget shook her head. "No one is here Abby. You were having a hallucination or something."

Tears welled up in my eyes and Bridget pulled me into her.

"Please don't tell Ian," I said into Bridget's shoulder, holding onto her tightly.

"Abby," she said, "I don't know what to do. I think we need to call Dr. Aldridge back."

"No, please." I pulled away and looked at her. "I think I've found someone who could help me, or at someone I could talk to about what has been going on. I found a job today. I'm pulling myself together. Just, please don't tell Ian about this."

Bridget looked at me carefully, studying me for a moment, and then nodded. "Okay."

The following morning, I made my way to the San Francisco Public Library around 7:30, so I would arrive on time at eight o'clock. As I walked up the steps, carrying my purse around my shoulder, I felt a sense of relief. It finally felt like something was going right in my life for the first time in a long time. My only hope was it would stay that way.

I made my way into the library, past the checkout desk, and back to the office area I had signed my paperwork in yesterday. When I walked in the room, Thomas was sitting at his desk, scribbling something down on a paper.

"I'm here for my first day," I announced.

He looked up and smiled. "Great! Here, have a seat."

He gestured to a chair next to his desk and I stepped forward and took it.

"Unfortunately," he continued, "I do not have any extra desks, so you are more than welcome to use mine when needed. I honestly don't use it very much at all; you've just happened to catch me at both of the times I've actually made use of it. The main thing I would like for you to do is keep track of the library's budget and supplies. You will be in charge of figuring out what expenses we have incurred every month and how much is left over to actually buy books, as well as keep up on the maintenance of some of our older selections. Does that sound okay for you?"

I nodded, even though I had secretly hoped I would be working with books directly. I could do bookkeeping all right, but my passion was books. Discovering them. Reading them. Collecting them.

But this would do for now.

Thomas spent the next hour showing me the process of keeping track of the library's budget and the organizational system for keeping track of bills, receipts, and any other necessities involving the budget of a library. He had just finished showing me the current budget when there was a knock outside. We both looked up to see the woman that had assisted me yesterday standing at the door.

"A Miss Hall is here to see you," she said to Thomas.

Thomas looked a bit annoyed at this declaration, but nodded and stood up. Before leaving he turned to me and said, "Why don't you begin subtracting these expenses from our current budget while I see to this matter?" He gestured toward a folder labeled *expenses* and then made his way out of the office. He pulled the door shut as he went, but it didn't catch and bounced back a little, allowing me to listen to the conversation outside.

"You haven't bothered to call me," a woman's voice, presumably the Miss Hall's, said.

"We discussed this, Shelly," Thomas responded. "I thought we agreed this was going to be casual?"

"I know," Shelly answered, switching from an annoyed tone to more of a cooing one. "But when I invited you into my bed, I had no idea how much I would come to need you."

My eyes grew wide and I looked up at the door. I felt as if I should get up and close it, but they'd surely hear that and know I'd overheard their clearly private and intimate conversation. Another part of me, one that had only blossomed in previous years, wanted to hear more.

"I'm not interested in a relationship, Shelly," Thomas replied. "I'm sorry."

I heard what sounded like a slap and then heels clicking against the floor, walking away.

Thomas came back into the office, shutting the door behind him.

"I'm assuming you heard that," he said, sitting back down in his chair, "considering the door was open."

"I apologize."

He gave me an odd look and then took a sip of water from the glass on his desk. "It isn't your fault. That actually happens quite a bit. I always tell women I'm not interested in more than one night, but sometimes they just don't listen." He leaned forward and put his face in his hands, sighing loudly. "My God, I can't believe I just said that to you. I do apologize."

"It's fine," I said back to him. I now remembered from the Timekeeper's Ball that there had been mention that the American Timekeeper was famous amongst the ladies. I now saw why, and I was rather curious. "Do you have lots of children?"

He burst out laughing at my comment. "I'm sorry?" he said,

trying to restrain himself. "Why would I have lots of children?"

"Oh, I just thought...." I responded, confused, color flooding my cheeks.

"There are—well, there are ways to—avoid that. Conception, I mean," Thomas said, now looking as uncomfortable as me.

I glanced at my lap, feeling foolish. Now that I thought about it, I'd heard whispers about such things.

"Abby, I don't mean to be rude, but I'm getting the feeling that you've lived a somewhat sheltered life. Am I correct?"

I swallowed and raised my gaze. "I suppose so."

I grabbed the expenses folder and began to subtract them from the budget as he had asked. I wasn't upset with him or anything. It was just that I had a longing for something more, for Phillip. By now, we would have been married. And the conversation I had just had with Thomas had reminded me of that. Maybe we would have had our own home. I imagined it—the perfect place; somewhere in the country. And in our home, we would have a library that housed the things we loved the most in this world besides our family and friends. Books.

As I continued to look over the materials in front of me, I heard Thomas stand up and come around behind me. A hand touched my shoulder and I looked up to see him looking at me.

"I apologize if I offended you with my comments," he said. "I just felt like you wanted an answer. I usually don't discuss such things."

"It's fine," I responded softly. "It wasn't really what you said that upset me." I thought about it for a moment, and then I decided to find out what he knew.

"What do you know about the reasons as to why I had to come to America?" I asked him.

He looked at me for a moment and then took a seat again behind his desk.

"Well," Thomas said, folding his hands in his lap, "I know what happened on the Tower Bridge, and other than that, I know that there was some kind of conflict of interest because Mathias is your father."

"I had a premonition," I told him. "I had a premonition that my fiancé, Phillip Hughes, was going to die in an air raid bombing and I went to try and save him." I did my best to choke back tears as I recounted the night of running to save Phillip, but they still came. I told Thomas how Mathias had not tried to stop me after I left. I told him how I had been running to save the man I loved, and how, on the way, I realized I couldn't. I also told him about the deaths of my parents. And before I knew it, I was spilling everything to him. Everything to this man I barely knew. Because he made me feel comfortable. He made me feel safe. And I hadn't felt safe in a long, long time. Not since Phillip.

When I was done speaking, Thomas handed me a handkerchief to dry my tears. He looked at me for a moment, considering me, before he spoke.

"I'm so sorry, Abigail. I've never known loss quite like that. My father is still alive, and when my mother passed away, it was expected. She suffered from an illness for a long time before she finally went. But to have so many of your loved ones die, so unexpectedly, and so near each other, I just can't imagine that. But I'm here for you. I want you to know that."

"Thank you," I responded, as I continued to dab at the pouring tears. "I better, um, get to subtracting these expenses."

Thomas smiled at me and nodded.

"Very well," he said. "I need to be off. Feel free to use my desk and chair, and if you need anything, remember that Gertrude is here to help as well."

I nodded at him, and he smiled again, stood up, and left the office.

I sat there wondering why I felt so comfortable around him. I had just poured out part of myself to him, and the scary part was that I was glad I had done it.

CHAPTER EIGHT

October 1944

The next several weeks passed in a blur; now that I was spending time working, the hallucinations were happening less. I also saw less of Bridget and Ian. As of yet, I still had not seen Ian at the library, so I continued to assume he used a different entrance to gain access to the Headquarters. October quickly arrived, and I worked at the library during the day and usually made my way home directly after. I realized it would be good for me to do more outside of the apartment, but I felt I was at least making a start at getting out more.

Thomas hadn't been lying when he said he was rarely at his desk. I could count on one hand the number of times he had been at his desk in the last three weeks, so usually, when I arrived in the morning, I chose to make myself right at home there, as he had said I could. When it all came down to it, the job wasn't that difficult. I simply needed to keep track of the budget and make sure that the library stayed within its monthly limits as far as budgeting needs were concerned.

I stood up to pour myself a glass of water from a pitcher that Thomas kept in the office. As I did so, I stopped breathing.

* * *

I was in the library, the San Francisco Public Library, but I was in the main room, near the checkout desk.

"Emily," a familiar voice said.

I turned and saw Gertrude, who was in charge of historical records, approaching a girl at the checkout desk.

"Yes, Ms. Francis?"

"I received Mr. Jane's permission to head out early tonight," Gertrude replied. "Do you think you'll be able to handle the counter for the rest of the evening?"

Emily smiled. "Of course, Ms. Francis. Have a lovely evening!"

"You do the same," said Gertrude, nodding at Emily and turning on her heel.

For whatever reason, I felt inclined to follow Gertrude out of the library and down the front steps, toward the street. She walked quickly, her purse clanging against her side as she moved.

Once at the bottom, she turned and looked both ways, waiting to cross the street. I looked around and saw a car going out of control, heading off the street and onto the path, toward the library and toward Gertrude. The car struck Gertrude, and she was thrown backward several feet.

Even from where I stood on the library steps, I could see she was dead.

"Miss Jordan."

I snapped out of my premonition and realized I was laying on the floor of Thomas' office, the pitcher of water shattered in pieces next to me. Luckily, none of the shards of glass had cut me, but my dress was wet with water.

"Miss Jordan?"

I looked up and was taken aback to find Gertrude standing in front of me. Gertrude. The woman about whom I had just had a premonition. The woman who was about to die.

"Y-y-yes?" I stuttered.

"Are you quite alright?"

She bent down and began picking up the pieces of glass on the floor. I quickly collected myself and did the same, tossing them in the trashcan by the door and then grabbing a handful of napkins that had been on the table with the pitcher and cleaning up the puddle of water on the floor.

"I'm alright," I said as I put the pieces in the trashcan. I looked up at her and added, "I'm sorry."

"For what?" Gertrude looked perplexed. "I just came to tell you I was leaving early and found you on the floor. Are you sure you're alright? You look quite pale."

I looked at her for a moment and then quickly looked away, trying not to let tears eclipse my vision.

"I'm fine," I said softly.

"Well, alright then."

I looked back and Gertrude stood, nodded at me, and then left the office, walking toward her death.

And here I sat, allowing another person to go out into the world and die. Another death I could prevent. But I couldn't. If I did, everyone else would suffer. I'm not sure what came over me in that moment. Perhaps I had seen too many people walk to their death, but I couldn't be compliant any longer. I stood up and began walking after Gertrude. She was already just outside the building.

I picked up my speed, but just as I was about to go through the door, a hand grabbed my arm and pulled me to a stop. I turned and found myself looking into Thomas' eyes.

"I'm not sure this is something you are thinking through," he said quietly.

I looked at him, aghast. He knew. Had he had the same premonition as I had?

A commotion from outside interrupted my thoughts. I heard people screaming and I quickly turned around to see the scene as it had occurred in my premonition come to life. Gertrude was dead in the street. People were running around, trying to get help. It was chaos. The clerk, Emily, came up to the door to see what was happening and she cried out.

Thomas quickly gathered himself and began to comfort Emily. The two of them walked out toward the street to see if there was anything they could do. I simply stood there, questioning my actions. If Thomas hadn't stopped me, I could have made a horrible mistake. A terrible mistake. He didn't know how horribly things could have gone, though. To him, he was just saving death from taking me instead. But really, he had saved the world and the lives of innocent people. I closed my eyes and took a deep breath, wondering what was happening to me.

The events of the previous day had been weighing on me heavily. I knew I couldn't go on ignoring them any longer. My inability to see things clearly almost caused me to make a decision that would affect innocent people. This was more than shell shock, as Dr. Aldridge had called it. There was something seriously wrong with me and I truly felt like it had to do with the world of the Timekeepers. I had to go back. I had to keep working in that world, and the only person I could trust to help me now was Thomas Jane.

I was sitting at my desk, working through some paperwork for Thomas while I waited for him to arrive for the day. I assumed he was down in the Headquarters, working on something to do with Timekeeping.

Footsteps could be heard outside the office door, and I quickly collected myself so I would be prepared for his arrival. The door opened and Thomas stepped into the office, giving me a wide grin.

"Thomas," I began, "there is something I need to talk to you about."

"You're ready to join us?" he responded.

I gave him a confused look and he simply added, "Premonition," while tapping his head.

"Well, I'm not sure what exactly your premonition showed you," I said, "but it's more than that. I really need to tell you the truth, so if you could sit for a moment, I will."

He did as I asked and I began pouring out everything to this man I had only known for a couple weeks. I started at the beginning, about how I had come into this world and how Mathias had originally lied to me and told me I would die if I hadn't. I told him how my mother wanted to keep me away from all of this and why it was now too late to stay away. I told him about the man who had approached me at the ball and told me that I was an original Timekeeper. I also explained how the voices had never really gone away; that even when they were full-fledged premonitions, I would still hear voices advising me not to do something or telling me I was a killer, and that I could no longer tell the difference between Timekeeping or if I was simply going mad. I explained the events that had been taking place recently and why I felt I now needed to return to this world.

Thomas simply sat there and took in everything I said. He didn't jump in and ask questions. He didn't stop me to offer his own suggestions. He just listened, and there was something refreshing in that.

"Thank you for telling me this," Thomas said when it was clear I was finished. "Did this Elijah tell you what the prophecy was about?"

I shook my head. "He only told me it was made thousands of years ago and it wasn't good. We didn't have a lot of time to hash out the details."

"Have you told anyone else about this…" Thomas stopped for a second, appearing to find the right word, "… *ability*, to continue hearing voices?"

"No," I said. "I honestly never thought about it. I wasn't thinking I should never hear voices again after I turned eighteen."

"But," Thomas went on, "the voices you have heard, are they yours? That's the *key* difference. Before, they were premonitions, just not fleshed out. You could only hear them, so they wouldn't be your voice. But if these voices speak in *your* voice—"

"They do," I said. "It has always been me, ever since I turned eighteen."

"Then I might have an idea of what is going on," Thomas said.

"I need the library. Follow me."

I followed Thomas out of the office, but was surprised when he walked in the opposite direction of the main library.

"I thought you said you needed the library?" I called after him.

"Not that kind of library."

I understood and followed Thomas to the end of the office hallway. He took out his set of keys and unlocked the door at the end, beckoning me to follow him. As soon as I stepped into the room beyond, he shut the door behind me, and relocked it. We were in what appeared to be a maintenance room. I laughed.

"What's so funny?" Thomas asked, making his way in front of me.

"Do we always hide our secret Headquarter entrances in the maintenance room?"

"Not always." He looked at me, gave me a wink, and then continued forward.

We walked deeper into the room and then stopped when we got to the middle. Thomas looked down at a rug on the floor, knelt down, and pulled it aside. In the rug's place was an intricate drawing of a clock, with an indent in the middle that looked just big enough to place a pocket watch into. Thomas pulled a pocket watch out of his shirt, unchained it from his neck, and placed it in the indent.

The sound of air pouring fourth, and stone grinding against stone, erupted into the room and the stone with the clock began to move aside into the wall, revealing a wide opening. Thomas stepped forward, where the stone had been, and began to walk down what I assumed to be stairs. He looked at me and then said, "Coming?" I broke my trance and followed him. We proceeded to make our way down a spiral staircase.

When we reached the bottom, the room we stepped into was a room that had not been at the London Headquarters. The London Headquarters had had shelves of books, but this room was an actual library. I gazed up to look at the vaulted ceilings above us, intricate designs of clocks were painted on the ceiling above. There were also pictures of men and women in long robes, pocket watches held by a long chain in their hands. The beauty of the paintings amazed me. The library itself was lined with shelves and shelves of books. I could smell the pages of the old, worn, and tattered books. It reminded me so much of the London Library, or what it used to be.

The other thing that caught my attention though, were the people hustling and bustling about. It wasn't just one person here and there, but person, after person, after person. It made me think I was in some sort of office building, with everyone moving around from place to place to complete their duties for the day.

"Who are all these people?" I asked.

Thomas gave me a quizzical look for a moment, but then comprehension came over his face.

"I forget that you've only been in the London Headquarters," he said. "Well, one of the reasons Mathias was never popular with the Council was because he insisted on doing everything himself. A normal Timekeeping Headquarters will generally have anywhere from fifty to a hundred people doing various duties, based on the size of the country."

"You mean all of these Timekeepers work for you?" I asked,

appalled that such a young man as Thomas had so many people under his command.

"In a sense yes, but I'm not your normal, everyday boss." Thomas winked at me again and then proceeded to head toward a section of books clearly labeled under "P."

As we made our way into the section, several people bustled past me, some even giving me a strange look.

"Some people are giving me strange looks," I said. "Do they know who I am?"

Thomas looked up and down the rows of shelves, trying to find whatever he was looking for. He spoke while continuing to look for a book. "Many of them have heard the story of what happened on the Tower Bridge in London. It caused quite a stir in our society, as so many were too daft to actually think that there could be evil Timekeepers. They all heard that you were supposed to be coming here eventually, so I'm sure many of them will make a guess at who you are. Found it!"

I looked over Thomas' shoulder to see him pull a thick, cloth-bound book from the shelf. It was pitch black, with the exception of gold letters on the spine and front that carried the same title: *Premonitions in Timekeepers*. I continued to look over his shoulder and watched as he flipped to a section titled "Telepathy."

"Telepathy?" I asked. I had heard the term before, but it was usually only something that came up in fictional books. "Isn't that—"

"It's when you can communicate with another person in your mind," Thomas said, cutting me off. He flipped through the pages of the chapter quickly. He had clearly read the book before, because he appeared to know what he was doing. "I had to do research," he continued, while still flipping the pages, "every Timekeeper does. You have to pick a specific area of study to concentrate on before you can successfully graduate from your training. My area was premonitions and in my research, I discovered a Timekeeper who had heard things that she thought were premonitions, but they weren't. It turned out it was—" he stopped speaking and made an exclamation of triumph. "Found it."

He turned the book around in his arms and pointed with an index finger at a passage that he wanted me to read. I stepped forward and began to read.

Telepathy in Timekeepers

The power of Telepathy is a curious one in the society of Timekeepers. It continues to befuddle researchers of the Timekeeping abilities, but evidence seems to suggest that the power only occurs between twins, both born with the Timekeeping ability. Initially, when first reported, the Timekeeper in question experienced voices she could interact with. These voices were in stark contrast to the previous voices she had heard (premonitions, before the eighteenth birthday), as they were clearly her own voice and there was also the component of interaction— a component not present in normal premonitions. It was later discovered that the Timekeeper had a long-lost twin, and the two had been separated at birth. Another interesting thing to note is that the power of telepathy is more noticeable in twins who are separated, rather than those that grew up together.

I looked up at Thomas. "You think I have a twin?"

"It's the only thing I can think of that would explain these other voices," he replied. "You've described everything perfectly—you are able to interact with them, they are your own voice. The only thing I can't wrap my head around is to why they would only begin after you turned eighteen. In everything I've read, it's something that should have been happening long before then. Regardless though, we need to find out what that prophecy is about."

"Timekeeper Jane."

We both looked to the end of the aisle of bookcases and saw a black girl, about my age, looking at us both.

"Yes, Alma?"

"The President is here to see you. He's in your office." She turned and walked away.

I looked up at Thomas in confusion. "The President?"

"Yes," Thomas replied. "He's been coming around a lot lately."

"You mean," I couldn't seem to get out what I was thinking, "the President of the United States?"

He gave me a weird grin. "Who else would I mean? Didn't your father at least tell you some significant non-Timekeepers know of our society?"

I racked my brain. He had said a lot, but he might have mentioned it.

"What does he need from you?" I asked.

"He's probably going to ask something about the war and America's involvement," said Thomas, walking away. "We can advise him on what to do, based on history. However, we most certainly cannot tell him what we know will happen. If you'll excuse me, Abigail. Please enjoy the library. I will be back soon and I can show you around if you'd like."

I nodded. "I would like that."

He smiled again, placed the book about premonitions back on the shelf, and walked away.

I turned and began to peruse the books about Timekeeping. Not everything was about Timekeeping though. There were subjects that were simply normal, non-Timekeeping subjects. I wondered what their purpose was other than to be read when in a Timekeeping library.

"Abigail?"

I turned and saw Ian walking to me from the other end of the aisle. As he did, I was reminded of the time we had met, almost a year ago now, at the London Library. He had approached me then, and he had called me *Melanie*. He had seemed confused for a moment, and then he had played it off like it was nothing. But what if it was something?

"Abigail," he said, inches away. "You're here. Did you change your mind? How did you know where to find the place?"

"It was all kind of coincidental actually," I responded. I quickly explained the story of how I had met Thomas at the Verdi Club, and then again, inadvertently, at the library when I had come looking for a job.

"That's great," Ian said, but there was something about his expression that suggested he thought otherwise. He probably thought I wasn't sane enough to handle it. "Would you like me to show you around?"

"Actually, I think Thomas is going to do that. He had to run off for a minute, but he'll be back in a bit."

"Very well." Ian considered me for a moment, as if he wanted to say or do something more, but he didn't. He walked around me and said he would see me later tonight. I was going to let him go, but I needed to know about him calling me Melanie.

"Ian?"

He turned around. "Yes?"

"Do you remember how we first met?"

Ian looked at the shelves of books around him and smiled. "If I recall, it was in the London Library."

"That's right," I said, stepping forward a bit. "And you called me Melanie at first? Do you remember that?"

It took him a moment to respond, but when he did, he simply said, "No, I don't recall doing that. I'll see you later." He turned on his heel and walked away. The unfortunate thing for Ian was that I knew him now. I had known him for almost a year. He had hesitated a moment too long when I asked him the question, and it was because of that, that I knew he was lying.

CHAPTER NINE

After Ian left, I decided to spend some time perusing the book Thomas had found about premonitions until he returned. It would at least get my brain off thoughts about Ian and his motives. I found a comfortable chair in the main center of the library and started reading the book from the beginning.

Most of the information at the beginning contained information I was already aware of, such as how premonitions wouldn't fully develop until a Timekeeper was eighteen. It still interested me, nevertheless.

"Find anything interesting?"

I looked up and found Thomas leaning over the chair, staring at the page I was on.

"It's the same book we were looking at earlier," I said.

He nodded and came around to sit in the chair next to me.

"How did things go with President Roosevelt?" I asked him.

"Like I said before, I advised him on some strategies he could implement, but when he asked about how the war would go, there was nothing I could tell him. They never like that answer. I get it though. It's hard to understand that we cannot change the course of history just because we want to, or because we want to save someone."

I knew that last part was a jab at me about yesterday.

"You didn't know until now though," I began, "that I technically *cannot* interfere with terrible things happening. Yesterday, you only assumed I would die. Why did you stop me?"

He sighed. "I'd like to say I'm used to it by now. I realize how young I am, but you aren't the first person I have been in charge of training. It's happened before and I've stopped them because that is the law. I knew Gertrude quite well, and I also knew that while her death was tragic, she's lived a long life. Why shouldn't you have the same?"

I looked away because I knew my eyes were beginning to water. I looked down at the book I was reading and tried to keep a sob from rising up within me, but it didn't work. I began to choke up.

"Hey," Thomas said, "I'm sorry. I didn't mean to upset you."

I looked at him as slow tears moved down my face. He looked like he wanted to pat me on the back, or give me some encouragement, but he also looked like he didn't want to invade my space. In the end though, he leaned in, his arms open, and I fell into his embrace. He held me like that, briefly, and then let me go.

"Thank you," I said.

He pulled a handkerchief out of his pocket and handed it to me. I dabbed at my eyes and attempted to pull myself together.

"So," I said, "when is the war going to end? If you can tell me, that is."

"It will be over within the next year," Thomas said. A feeling of joy erupted in me, but also sadness, because we had another year of war. "But Abigail, so many more terrible things are going to happen before then. It's not going to be pretty. But anyway, as I was walking out, I saw you talking to Ian. So, does he know now?"

I nodded. "He does. And I'm not sure if I trust him."

"Why do you say that?" Thomas asked.

I took a deep breath, collecting myself, and then began to tell Thomas everything that had been happening with Ian lately. I started with his change in attitude since we had arrived in America. I also told him how he didn't seem to mind that I wasn't coming to training and how I felt that was a little out of character for him. And finally, I told him about what I had remembered today. About when Ian had called me Melanie, and how he had brushed it off when I had confronted him about it.

"I want you to be careful around him," Thomas said after I was finished. "I don't want to jump to conclusions and assume the worst of people, but just do me a favor and be careful. Okay?"

I nodded.

"Good," he said, standing up. "Follow me, and I will show you the rest of the place."

"Let me put this back first," I said. I quickly went back to the aisle that we had found the book on premonitions on and placed it back in its slot.

You are a killer.

I tensed and looked around. It was the voice. My voice. The one that had been speaking to me. Why would my twin, if I truly had one, want to say these things to me?

You are a killer, it said again. *And you will pay.*

I closed my eyes a moment, took a deep breath, and then opened them again. There was nothing but silence. I could get through this. I walked out of the book section I was in and followed Thomas to the next part of the Headquarters.

Thomas led me through the various rooms of the San Francisco Headquarters such as the ballroom, the guest rooms, and also some private conference rooms that were used when meeting with important officials, either from the Council or from actual government officials. I continued to be amazed by the hustle and bustle of people moving about the Headquarters when compared to the rather quiet atmosphere of the London Headquarters.

"I just can't get over all of the people," I said to Thomas. "It really makes me feel like Mathias isn't in the best place right now. He's consumed in his work and refuses to let others in. I'm his daughter and it was hard, even for me, to gain a sense of trust with him. Plus, I kept suspecting him all the time because of the way he acted, when in actuality he was just trying to protect me."

"Well," Thomas replied, "as I said before, Mathias is unfortunately known for being reclusive. I honestly wouldn't be surprised if the Council tries to step in soon and retire him from his duties."

I looked at him, surprise written all over my face. "You think they'd do that?"

"Oh, yes," Thomas added. "Unfortunately, even with Winston gone, Mathias still isn't liked amongst those in the Council."

I shook my head in frustration. "They just don't understand him.

If they did, if they'd really take a moment to understand what he's been through, I think they would see things differently."

Thomas nodded. "Perhaps. Have you spoken to him recently?"

"I've sent letters," I responded. "But he's never written back. I don't know if he's trying to just avoid me, or if he's upset with me. Even I still can't understand everything about him."

"If you'd like," Thomas said, "I can show you how to reach him directly. You could send a direct message with your pocket watch."

Another look of surprise crossed my face. "You can send a message with the pocket watch?"

Thomas laughed. "I've got quite a bit to teach you, I see. But yes, you can send messages with the pocket watch. That is your main tool as a Timekeeper. You never want to be without it. Speaking of it, do you have yours with you? I need to program it so that you will be connected with those here at the San Francisco Headquarters."

I pulled out my pocket watch and handed it to him. He opened it and started messing with some dials inside it. He leaned over to show me what he was doing as he did so.

"If you flip this dial here," Thomas said, gesturing to the right side of the pocket watch, "you can change it from a clock to an alphabet. And then you just use the dials that you would use to set the time to type in your message. At the beginning of your message, simply put attention to and the name of the Timekeeper. You want to be wary though. All messages are sent directly to the Central Headquarters, monitored, and then processed.

"A Timekeeper at Central Headquarters will read your message, censor it if necessary, and then send it on to the appropriate party.

This is why you receive your pocket watch from the Council. They calibrate everything at the Central Headquarters and then send everything on to the appropriate party."

"You said they censor the messages?" I asked.

"Yes," Thomas said. "Therefore, you don't want to send anything, well, inappropriate. It's okay for you to send a simple message to Mathias asking why he hasn't been communicating, but in most cases, you should simply use the messaging on the pocket watch for Timekeeping-related purposes."

"How is this all possible?" I asked.

"It all has to do with the Time Line," Thomas responded. "All of our Time Lines are created from the main Time Line at the Central Headquarters. All of that energy, or whatever you want to call it, well it's all connected. And supposedly, that energy comes from the original Time Line, which again has never been found, but what you've told me indicates otherwise. But that's a discussion for another day. I need to show you my study. Follow me."

Thomas handed me back the pocket watch and then led me down the hallway we were in to a set of large, oak double doors at the end. As soon as he reached them, he pushed them open rather dramatically. The room they led into was breathtaking. Books upon books lined the shelves along the walls.

"You have two libraries?" I asked.

"Two is always better than one," he replied.

I smiled and admired the large fireplace that stood at the center of the room, a fire crackling in the grate. At various places in the room were cushy leather chairs and couches that looked like they would be quite comfortable. In the middle of the room was a long table with several chairs. I assumed it to be some kind of conference table where Thomas would have meetings. And of course, just by the fireplace was Thomas' wooden desk. It looked as if it had been hand-crafted. I was making my way to it when a glint from above the fireplace caught my eye. I looked up to see a long sword hanging beautifully on the wall.

I looked at Thomas and gestured toward the sword. "Can I ask about that?"

"It's a family heirloom," Thomas replied. "My grandfather, Reginald Jane, fought in the Civil War. He came back with that sword and I've always kept it."

"Timekeepers fought in the war?" I asked.

"Not exactly," Thomas said. "I never knew my birth mother. She and my father married, had me, and then she left. She was the Timekeeper whereas my father was not. After she left, her father needed someone to pass the Headquarters on to so that they could technically keep it in the family and pass it on to me. So they initiated my father into Timekeeping. It's rare, but it can be done. My father did it for as long as he needed to, trained me, and now, here I am."

I had thought he had told me previously that his mother had died, but I didn't question it at the moment. It also didn't feel like the time to question him on what might be a sensitive subject. So, I decided to inquire about all of the people bustling about.

"What about all of these other people?" I asked. "Don't they have families and Headquarters they will run someday?"

Thomas shook his head. "Not every Timekeeper will end up

running a Headquarters. Some will serve as assistants, some will work on the Council, and others might do those jobs that must be done, such as monitoring and censoring messages sent via pocket watch."

I laughed. "That sounds awful."

"I suppose it probably would be," Thomas said. "Now, how about we take a look at the Time Line."

Thomas led me through a door at the side of the room and we were suddenly in a long hallway that stretched a long way. At the very end, I could see the Time Line, a constant, solid blue like the one in London, floating in midair. Directly behind us was a set of stairs.

"Where do those lead?" I asked.

"Another entrance," Thomas said. "Those stairs will take you out through the San Francisco Ferry Building."

I nodded and followed Thomas down the hallway. When we arrived at the end, he reached out and slid the Time Line with his fingers so it went through all the various dates in the history of America.

"Well," Thomas said, taking a step back, "I believe that is everything."

"Timekeeper Jane."

We both turned to see the same girl from earlier walking down the hallway. She smiled at me as she approached and then turned her attention to Thomas.

"Alma," Thomas said, "please call me Thomas. Timekeeper Jane is so formal."

Alma giggled and then said, "Councilor Keaton is in conference room two for you. She wanted a briefing about your meeting with

President Eisenhower."

Thomas nodded and then turned to me. "Well, this is where I will leave you Abigail. Feel free to explore some more, of if you'd like to return to your job, you're more than welcome."

My job. I had almost forgotten I had a job I needed to be doing in the San Francisco library. Thomas turned to walk away, but then turned back again.

"Abigail?"

I looked at him.

"Would you care to join me for a night out? Nothing special, just to get to know each other. I thought we could go out tomorrow, after you get off at the library."

A night out. I knew I was probably giving him a strange look, but I quickly tried to hide it. As much as a part of me felt like I shouldn't, I told him I would. He smiled and walked away, leaving me there with Alma.

"I didn't introduce myself earlier," Alma said, holding out her hand. "I'm Alma James. I'm Thomas' back-up when he isn't here."

"Abigail Jordan," I said, shaking her hand. "So you're going to take over once Thomas retires?"

Alma laughed at that. "I was only joking. I'm like you, a Timekeeper in training. However, I haven't been fully initiated yet. In regards to your question though, I would love to do that one day, but that would only happen if he didn't have any children. Otherwise, it would go to them, unless they didn't want it. They really like to keep things in the family in the Timekeeping world. And I really don't think Thomas is going to have a problem finding a wife to have children with someday."

She started laughing again and I did too. But based on what I knew about him, I did wonder if that was something he wanted.

"Well," Alma said, "I need to be getting back. It was nice meeting you. Please let me know if there is anything at all that you need. I've been here a while now and at least know where most things are."

I smiled and nodded and she walked away, leaving me alone.

You are a traitor.

My body went cold as I looked around the room for the voice, knowing I'd find nobody there with me.

What would Phillip think if he saw you now? It hasn't even been a year and you're already running off with another man.

Deep breaths. That was what I needed to do. I closed my eyes and took a long, deep breath. When I opened them again, the voice, or my voice, was gone.

That evening I managed to arrive home after Bridget for once. When I entered the apartment, she was in the kitchen preparing dinner. I could hear pots and pans clanging away as I made my way into the kitchen. She looked up as I entered.

"Hey, there."

I smiled at Bridget and took a seat at our small table.

"What's for dinner?" I asked.

"I'm just throwing together some stir fry," Bridget responded. "Ian and I had lunch today. He tells me he ran into you at the American Headquarters?"

News travels fast apparently.

"That's right," I responded. "I felt like it was finally time to go back and I also think Thomas might be able to help with some of the problems I've been having lately."

"How so?"

"He thinks that while some of it may be because of the trauma I've experienced, some of it might also be because of Timekeeping." I launched into an explanation about what we had found out in the library about my premonitions and possible telepathy. Bridget's eyes grew wider as I mentioned the possibility of having a twin.

"Mathias never mentioned any of this to you?" she asked in response.

"No," I responded. "And honestly, I don't think he knows. My biological mother left their secret Headquarters to have me and never returned. There would be no way of knowing she was pregnant with twins. Except for maybe a premonition."

"Are you going to contact Mathias and ask him about it?"

I shook my head. "I've tried contacting him and he hasn't responded to any of the letters I've written."

Bridget's face changed into one of suddenly remembering something. She stepped out of the kitchen for a moment and then quickly returned, an envelope in her hand.

"Usually Ian gets the post," she said, "but since I was home early, I picked it up and I noticed a letter for you from London."

My heart began beating anxiously as I reached out for the letter. I clutched it and began tearing it open immediately. After eight long months, Mathias had finally written me back. I hoped it contained answers to some of the questions that I had asked him.

Dear Abigail,

I understand that you are probably angry with me, even though I had thought we made amends before you left London. I so desperately wish you would respond to my letters. It is getting rather lonely here without anyone to talk to, especially now that I no longer have Ian. I suppose the time has come that I should finally consider bringing in some other Timekeepers to help run the place.

I hope that you are finding solace in your new home, even if you aren't pursuing Timekeeping at the current time. Councilor Headrick informed me of your decision shortly after you arrived in San Francisco. Please understand that I am truly sorry for how I previously acted, and I hope to hear from you soon.

Love,

Mathias

I looked up at Bridget in confusion. "I don't understand."

"What do you mean?" she asked, continuing to stir the skillet on the stovetop.

"He's acting like he hasn't gotten any of my letters," I responded. "He's asking why I haven't responded to his letters, and this is the first one that I've gotten from him."

Bridget looked at me, a look of confusion on her face as well. "Maybe they've been intercepted and weren't sent along?"

"Every single one?" I asked. "Not only mine, but his as well?"

"That is odd," Bridget said. "I honestly have no idea. You should write back though. Maybe you can run down and get it sent off tonight?"

I nodded. That would probably be a good idea. I found pen and paper and quickly began to write.

Dear Mathias,

I'm not sure what to make of your letter. I've sent you several letters in the past eight months and you act as if you've never gotten them. The letter that I just received from you was the first letter I have gotten from you. S,o either our mail has been intercepted, or something else is going on.

Anyway, I'm doing okay here in San Francisco. I've been struggling though. I've had dreams about Phillip and my parents, and it often ends with them accusing me of killing them. I have decided to seek help from Thomas Jane and will probably continue my studies. I won't say much in this letter. I just want to make sure you get it. Write back quickly.

Love,

Abigail

The door to the apartment opened and shut as I signed my name. Ian walked into the kitchen.

"Evening ladies," he announced, quickly crossing the kitchen and giving Bridget a kiss on the lips. He turned to me and sat down at the table. "Sending off another letter? Leave it on the counter and I'll get it when I go out in the morning."

"I'm actually going to just run it down and get it sent off now," I responded. "Bridget got the post today and I finally got a letter from Mathias. He acts as if I haven't sent him anything and also asks if I've gotten his previous letters."

I stood up, took the letter, and grabbed my coat hanging on the wall hook.

"Abby," Ian says, "you've had a long day with everything at the Headquarters. I'll run that letter down for you. You stay here and rest."

"No, it's okay. I really want to make sure this one gets out."

Ian reached out his hand for the letter. "No, really, Abby. I insist."

I gave Ian a questioning look before it all dawned on me. How could I have been so stupid? Ian had been the one handling all of the correspondence. He had sent out every single one of my letters because I hadn't wanted to leave the apartment. He had been the person in charge of getting the post every day. Today was the first day, in probably all of the time that we had been here, that Bridget had gotten home early enough to get it.

"No," I said firmly, shaking my head. "Thank you, Ian, but I will get this delivered."

I put the letter in the pocket of my coat and quickly walked out of the apartment. Bridget had given us both a questioning look, but turned back to her stir fry. I knew now that Ian had been keeping my letters from me. Why? I didn't know. There were things that didn't line up, but I needed more proof before I could say anything to Bridget about it. And if it was proof I needed, I would get it.

As soon as I was on the street, I crossed over to the nearest mailbox and placed the letter safely inside. I had a strong inclination that Mathias would get this one.

CHAPTER TEN

As the day slowly ticked by, my mind was focused on the same three things. First, Thomas had asked me out on a date and we would be going out after I was off today. Second, Ian had been the one handling my letters, none of which had gotten to Mathias. Third, there was a prophecy about me, and apparently a twin sister that I knew nothing about. I did my best to not let these thoughts consume me, but as I had already verified the budget for the day and cleaned Thomas' office entirely, there wasn't much else for me to do except to sit and think. Thomas had yet to show up for work. Even though this was usually how he conducted his days, a part of me felt like he was rethinking his proposal the previous evening. I laughed out loud at that.

"I'm sitting here worrying about be being rejected," I said to the room. I felt selfish for it, but I also felt grateful. It felt... well it felt *normal* to sit here and think about being rejected instead of focusing on the thoughts that were constantly pouring into my head, causing me unwanted anxiety. If it was my sister doing the talking, why would a sister do that? Where was she? Why did she dislike me so much? But the answer to that went to the grave with my mother. Only she knew what happened that night. If she had twins, she left one of us with the sisters at St. Agnus's Orphanage in London. Or maybe she had left both of us? As soon as this thought crossed my mind, Thomas walked through the doorway.

"I need to go to London," I immediately said.

He stopped abruptly, clearly surprised, and gave me a questioning look.

"Well that'll be a little difficult," he said. "You'll have to go the way you came and that won't be cheap."

I shook my head. "No. I need to get there now. Can we travel through the Time Line?"

"Travel through the Time Line has to be approved in advance by the Council," Thomas responded.

"And what happens if it isn't? Can they stop us from going?"

Thomas looked wary at this. I could tell he wanted to help me, but I could also tell that he didn't want to get us into any trouble either.

"Well, no," he finally said. "But they will know that we did it. An alert will come up on their end and we will be questioned."

"Thomas, I really need you to help me with this. I need to go to the orphanage that I was left at and ask them if they knew anything about me having a twin."

Thomas looked away and then began pacing the room, clearly thinking through my request. He looked like he wanted to fight me on it, but he also looked like he was fighting himself on it. Finally, after rubbing his hands through his hair and sighing, he looked at me and nodded.

"Fine," he said. "Let's go, now."

I followed him before he could change his mind.

The long narrow hallway that led to the Time Line stood in front of us. I could see it glowing at the end, floating above ground. It was almost as if it was waiting for us to come to it and use it. As we approached, Thomas reached into his pocket and pulled out his pocket watch. He opened it and began to move some dials.

"First," he said, "you need to set it to travel, and then you put in your location. A map of the world will appear, and you can select your location. It can be broad, such as the United Kingdom for example, but if you do that, you will end up wherever it takes you. For now, we will narrow in on a certain location." He hit a button on the side of his pocket watch that read "travel" and just as he said it would, a map appeared. It was like the Time Line; it was made up of some sort of energy that floated from out of the pocket watch. Thomas selected the United Kingdom, and then narrowed in on the London Headquarters, which was clearly marked on the map.

"And then," he continued, outstretching his arm, the pocket watch just barely touching the energy of the Time Line, "you touch the Time Line and go."

He quickly grabbed my hand, lowering the pocket watch as he did, and the room around us began to dissolve completely. For a moment, we were standing on nothing. It was as if we were floating in space, with nothing around us except blackness, but then, slowly, the London Headquarters began to materialize around us and I found myself in the room, just beyond Mathias' study. I had only been here once, when Mathias had first trained me on parts of the

Time Line, but I remembered it. Directly behind us was the small opening that would lead out through the fireplace and into the study which would then lead to the hallway and up through the exit in the Parliament building. Before we could even move, footsteps were heard, and Mathias, my biological father, stood before us.

The sight of him sent my heart racing. He looked even worse than when I had seen him last. He was skinnier, almost to the point where it looked as if he was unhealthy. His hair was longer, coming close to being past his shoulders, and he really needed to trim his beard. It was growing wildly in different directions.

He looked from Thomas and then to me and then ran forward and pulled me into him. He held me like that for what felt like hours, until he finally pulled away.

"I thought I heard someone come in," he said to us. "You got a visit approved?"

Guilt seeped into me. He thought I was visiting him.

"Not exactly," I said, looking at Thomas.

"Mathias," Thomas said, outstretching his hand. "I don't think we've had the pleasure of meeting. I'm Thomas Jane."

Mathias took it. "Well, you tend to not show up to anything."

"Because he's the only one that does that," I muttered, brushing past the two of them and into the study. I immediately found my familiar spot on Mathias' couch and sat down. Thomas followed me and took a seat next to me, with Mathias sitting behind his desk.

Thomas beat me to explaining our visit. "We didn't get this visit approved, Mathias. There will no doubt be someone calling soon, so I think it would be best if you would come with us. We needed to come to London to do a bit of—" he hesitated, clearly unsure of what exactly to say. Finally, Thomas simply said, "A bit of research."

Mathias nodded. I could tell he knew there was more to this, but he was clearly willing to help us out.

"Let me get my coat," he said. "It'll be nice to get out for a change."

As Mathias went to find his coat, a part of me worried he had not been out since I left.

The three of us made our way to the tube and boarded the train that would take us to the closest exit to St. Agnus's. I was surprised to find it was now dark, whereas when I had left San Francisco it had been in the early afternoon. Then, I remembered the time difference.

I had no idea if our journey would be worth it, but I was appreciative Mathias was with us and we could fill him in and question him along the way. As we sat in the train car, amidst some questioning stares at Mathias' unkempt appearance, I filled him in on everything that had happened. I told him about the letters I had been sending, but that had apparently not been sent. This was also new information to Thomas, as I hadn't had the chance to tell him yet today.

I informed Mathias of my suspicions about Ian as well as his sudden change in behavior. Finally, we got to the part about what we found out in regards to my possibly having a sister who was communicating with me telepathically. When I finished, Mathias sat back, eyes wide, and stared ahead.

The train continued to rumble on and Mathias simply sat there in silence. Finally, he sighed and looked back at me.

"Well," he began, "for Ian, I don't know what to say. I've known the boy for years. I trained him. Never once has he acted suspicious to me. Please, don't think I'm saying you're wrong or aren't telling the truth. I believe you about what you've seen. I'm just saying I have no idea as to why he would be acting this way.

"And as for a twin sister, I honestly have no idea. Your mother never once said anything about carrying twins, even in the letters she left me."

Thomas leaned forward, a curious expression on his face. "Going back to Ian, how did he come to train at the London Headquarters? Do you know his family?"

Mathias had a quizzical expression on his face. He carefully pondered this question before he finally answered. "Honestly, I can't say I know much about the boy. He was brought to me by Councilor Headrick. Now that I recall, it was a rather unusual situation. Usually training with a Timekeeper is planned months in advance. Headrick showed up one day with the boy, told me he needed to be trained, and she left it at that."

"Why does everything seem to involve her?" I asked both Thomas and Mathias. "Surely there are other councilors that handle things, but everything, at least from my end of things, seems to be coming from her."

"So many things we didn't get around to training you on," Mathias mumbled. "Headrick was the assigned councilor to Europe, that is before the death of Winston. Now she's leading up the Council, which for all intents and purposes would mean she's the boss of us all. Before that though, she would handle all official business with the Timekeepers in each country within the continent. Every continent is assigned a different councilor that oversees the business of each country's Headquarters."

"That's right," Thomas confirmed. "You heard yesterday about my meeting with Councilor Keaton. She's assigned to North America."

"You said Headrick replaced Winston," I repeated to Mathias. He nodded at me. "If that's the case, then why wouldn't there have been someone else to oversee me going to America? Why her? Surely she had enough going on that such a minor thing as transferring a Timekeeper in training could be pawned off on someone else?"

Mathias didn't know how to answer this. He considered it for a moment before finally saying, "I honestly can't say."

"Abigail," Thomas said, "what are you implying? Are you suggesting our leader is working against us?"

Was that what I was suggesting? I honestly didn't know. I just didn't understand why Headrick would be so concerned with the minor task of transferring a Timekeeper when she was in charge of everything. It would be like the president of the United States getting involved with a state issue when there were clearly governors who could handle the situation.

"I don't know," I finally said to Thomas. "But something isn't right."

Before either of us could respond, the train came to a screeching halt as we arrived at our destination. I tucked away my thoughts as we ascended the stairs to make our way to St. Agnus's.

* * *

Sister Margaret, the same nun who had assisted both Ian and I months ago, opened the door of the orphanage when we called. She looked from Mathias, to Thomas, and then finally to me, a smile widening on her face as she remembered.

"Abigail," she said. "It's a pleasure to see you, but I have to say I can't seem to understand why you're back. I told you all I knew the last time."

"I know, Sister," I responded, "but I wanted to see if I could press you a little more. I've recently found out a few things and I think it would be of the utmost importance to retrace all of my mother's steps from that night."

A saddened look dawned on Sister Margaret's face. She quickly nodded and beckoned for us to come in. We followed her into the building, familiarity hitting me hard. The last time I was here my parents had been alive. Phillip had been alive. I brushed aside the thoughts and began to follow Sister Margaret as she led us into her office. But I stopped in the hallway, my attention drawn to the wall that was adorned with photographs of the sisters and the children from the orphanage. It looked like they had one for every year. I stepped forward and looked directly at a photograph that was taken not too many years ago. A nun in it looked familiar. Before I could question it further, Sister Margaret interrupted me.

"We take one every year out in the country," she said. "We take the children out there to get away from the city for a bit. As you can see, many of them are never adopted out. For some, this is where they grow up. It's quite sad. Please, follow me."

I didn't look back at the picture as Sister Margaret led us into her office, but my mind was still racing at what I had seen. I took a seat in front of her desk, Thomas and Mathias behind me.

"Again," Sister Margaret said as she sat down, "I'm not sure what more there is I can help you with, but I will try my best."

I didn't hesitate to start explaining. "I've recently come to learn I might have a twin sister." Sister Margaret's face immediately transformed into one of shock and disbelief, but she allowed me to continue my story. I altered things a bit so as to leave out any evidence of being a Timekeeper, but I explained that we believed my mother had been keeping secrets and that she had given birth to twins that night.

"I guess I was wondering if you could give an account of exactly what happened that night," I finally said. "I want to know everything, or as much as you can possibly remember."

"Abigail," Sister Margaret said, "again, I'm afraid there isn't anything more to say. Your mother came to us with you in her arms and left you with us. She demanded we find you a home and that was it."

If my mother were here, Annette Jordan that is, she would have a fit at what I was about to say. But it needed to be said and I looked Sister Margaret straight into her eyes as I said it.

"You're lying."

Sister Margaret looked like I had slapped her. "Excuse me?"

I felt a hand on my shoulder and Thomas spoke. "Abigail, what are you doing?"

I looked at Mathias and Thomas, and then answered. "I'm not

doing anything. She's lying."

Immediately I stood up and walked back into the main hallway, reaching up and pulling down one of the photographs nailed to the wall.

"Miss Jordan," Sister Margaret began, "I'm very sorry about your predicament, but that does not give you the right to come into this orphanage and have your way with the place."

Picture in hand, I marched back into the office and showed it to Mathias, my finger on the nun that had caught my attention earlier.

"Is this my mother?" I asked him.

Mathias studied the picture carefully, and then a look of bewilderment came onto his face as he nodded. I then turned and planted the picture down in front of Sister Margaret and pointed out the nun in question.

"There are only a few scenarios here, Sister," I said. "The first is that you are lying, the second is that my mother was a nun here and you were completely oblivious to that fact which I find highly unlikely, and the third is that there is another woman walking around with my mother's face. Which scenario is it and is this nun still here?"

Sister Margaret looked visibly upset. I had caught her in the act and I suddenly felt quite guilty about it. Whatever her reason for lying to me in the past, her expression was now telling me that it might have been necessary. And I hated that I was forcing her to tell me what her reason was, but I truly needed to know. She sighed and then looked at me.

"I made a confidence a very long time ago with your mother," Sister Margaret finally said. "It was a confidence I swore I would never break. And I knew if I'd have to lie to keep it, I would."

I sat down again and looked directly at Sister Margaret, and then I reached forward and grabbed her hand. She didn't pull away from me, and she didn't seem surprised by the gesture either.

"I have no idea what you know," I told her, "but I think my mother made you swear not to break this confidence to keep me safe. I believe she was trying to protect me from the world she knew, and unfortunately that didn't happen. She never wanted me to meet my biological father, Mathias."

I gestured toward Mathias and then continued. "However, I have. So, truly, from the bottom of my heart, I do not think this confidence matters anymore. I think it is imperative you tell me what you know, because in the end, that is what is probably going to protect me more now."

By this point, tears had begun to form in Sister Margaret's eyes. She pulled out a handkerchief and began to dab at the moisture. Finally, she put the handkerchief down and spoke.

"The woman in the picture is not your mother," she said. "The woman is your mother's sister, Eleanor Callaghan. From what I understand, your mother and Eleanor were identical twins and their brother was their fraternal twin, making them triplets. Eleanor was a devout Catholic nun and she came from a troubled home life. She had a strained relationship with her sister, your mother. She did, however, speak fondly of her brother. She mentioned him numerous times. If I remember correctly, I believe he was called Elijah."

Elijah. It was as if a door that had always been locked in my head had suddenly been unlocked. Elijah, the man I met at my initiation—

the man who had answered so many of my questions, but left me with even more—was my mother's brother. My uncle. I wanted to find a quiet place to ponder this revelation, but Sister Margaret was still speaking, and I needed to listen.

"Eleanor disagreed with what she always referred to as the family practice. She never mentioned what it was that the Callaghan family did, or were expected to continue on in as they grew older, but for whatever reason, she vehemently disagreed with it. She said they always talked about power. She believed there was too much power and too much evil, which is why she found solace in her Catholic faith. I first met Eleanor in church, and the two of us went through the process of discernment together. We would often spend time praying together, determining whether or not becoming a nun was what God was calling us to do. Finally, we made the decision to join a convent together, which eventually led us to running this orphanage together."

Sister Margaret took a momentary break in her story and reached forward to pour herself a glass of water from a pitcher on her desk. After taking a few sips, she continued.

"Eleanor informed me that Elisabeth had been married. Apparently, she had not been invited and had respected this decision. Eventually, Elisabeth became pregnant. Throughout her pregnancy, Elisabeth would spend quite a bit of time here with her sister. I have no idea why she did this, I just know she was here. One night, about a week before your birth, Eleanor informed me Elisabeth needed to give up her baby and asked if I could find a suitable family immediately. I questioned as to whether this was truly what Elisabeth wanted, as it couldn't be undone once the process was complete. Eleanor begged me and I finally agreed.

"The night you were born, the woman that dropped you off was dressed as a nun, wearing Eleanore's clothes, but it wasn't Eleanor. It was Elisabeth. I know it deep in my marrow, and it continues to haunt me to this day that I didn't reach out and ask what was going on. I simply pretended as if she had fooled me, and maybe she knew she wasn't fooling me. I honestly cannot say. Maybe the disguise was for someone else, but regardless of that, when you work closely with a woman for so many years, you can tell them apart from their twin, even when they are identical. I had seen them together enough times to know which was which. The woman dressed as a nun was your mother, not Eleanor. And it was Eleanor who was found hanging from that bridge."

"How could you know that?" I gasped.

"This was not in the papers, but I work with closely with Scotland Yard when it comes to the children under my care. I asked about the woman they had found, and the inspector told me her autopsy showed no signs of having given birth, or having even been pregnant for that matter. The woman that died that day was Eleanor. For all I know, your mother is still alive."

The room was so silent in that moment all we could hear were the creaks of the old building as it moaned from the wind. I was looking at Sister Margaret, but I wasn't *really* looking at her. I was thinking about my biological mother. She was alive, or at least she hadn't died *that* night. I also thought of my aunt. This woman I had never met had sacrificed her life, presumably, to protect her sister and her sister's child. And there was also Elijah, who I knew now to be my uncle. But there was still the matter of *my* twin sister, and Sister Margaret hadn't touched on that.

"What about my twin?" I finally asked. "Do you know if my mother had twins?"

"That I cannot say. I honestly do not know, and if your mother did have twins, I have no idea why you would have been the only one who was dropped off that night. The only thing I can say is I fulfilled my end of the agreement by finding you a home immediately. What I told you before about your mother saying you needed to be named Abigail, well I told you the truth about that. Your mother also indicated I not speak of your adoption to anyone. Honestly, I almost didn't say anything to you when you came the last time, but I knew it was you. I could tell. You look so much like your mother, and your aunt, for that matter. Anyway, Dean and Annette Jordan were generous donors to our orphanage for years and they were first on the list to be contacted about a new baby, and that's where your story began. As for your mother and Eleanor, I never saw either of them again."

The room was silent as we all took in the story Sister Margaret had just relayed. Questions were being processed in my head and the only thing I could think to ask about was the confidence Sister Margaret had vowed to keep.

"You said you swore you wouldn't tell anyone this," I said. "How did that come about?"

"Your mother, even though she was dressed as Eleanor, made me swear to the story that it was your mother who dropped you off here, insisted you be placed with a family, and that was the end of it. And obviously, she left the letter to give to your adoptive parents. And even that particular story she wanted kept between your adoptive parents and myself. If anyone came knocking, asking about you or throwing around your mother or aunt's name, I was to act as if I didn't know about any of it. She also insisted I never speak to anyone about my relationship with Eleanor. At that point, not knowing what was to come, I had pretty much come to the conclusion I would probably never see Eleanor again."

I finally stood up, as I felt Sister Margaret had told us everything she knew.

"Thank you so much," I said to her.

She looked at me and smiled before standing herself. She led us to the door, opened it, and we stepped out onto the street. I nodded at Sister Margaret and smiled. She returned the smile and then closed the door.

CHAPTER ELEVEN

By the time we had returned to the London Headquarters, it was almost ten in the evening. I smiled knowing it would only be two in the afternoon when we returned to San Francisco. Thomas and I took a seat on Mathias' couch, with Mathias once again taking a seat behind his desk and gazing at us, contemplating, as he had done all those months ago when I first started to know him.

"Do you think she's alive?" I asked, breaking the silence. "She obviously didn't die on the bridge."

Mathias put his head in his hands and took a deep breath before looking back up at me. "I have no idea Abigail. I want to believe she is. I want to believe she's been out there all this time, trying to protect us. But I also don't want to be put the through the experience of losing her again. If she were alive, I cannot understand why she wouldn't contact me. Why wouldn't she ask for my help in all of this?"

"Because she's protecting us," I responded. "It's what she's been doing all this time."

I could understand him not wanting to go through this again though. If there were any way Phillip were suddenly alive, or my parents, I wouldn't want to get my hopes up. But I also felt in this situation we needed to find out more information about my mother and the family from which she came.

"We need to find Elijah," I finally said. "The only time I've seen him was when he showed up at my initiation ceremony. He might be the key to everything. The only thing is, he never gave me any way for me to contact him. Did my mother leave anything behind? Anything at all? Maybe something that contained information about her family?"

Mathias shook his head at me. "When it was only me down here, after she died, I went through everything. This was while I was still at the old Headquarters. Your mother never had anything here with the exception of the clothes she had left behind. As I'm sure you've gathered, she was a very secretive woman."

"Wait," I said, realization hitting me. "I do have something of my mother's. At least, I'm fairly certain it's hers. Bessie left it for me when we she was luring me into the old headquarters. It was a pocket watch and I had to use it in order to get into the place. I forgot about it after everything that happened, but I still have it. It's with my things in San Francisco. Thinking about it now, though, it might actually belong to Eleanor if she is the one who ran into Bessie that night."

"I could look at it when we get back," Thomas added. "Perhaps there is some way we could use it to communicate with Elijah?"

I nodded at the idea as the room behind the fireplace suddenly flashed, followed by a whooshing sound. I heard footsteps and then Councilor Headrick walked out, her face stern.

"Timekeeper Jane," she said, skipping over any formal introductions, "you did not alert the Council of this travel assignment, which as I know you are aware, is strictly forbidden."

Thomas immediately stood up, a look of shame appearing on his face. "My apologies, Councilor. I suppose I let emotion cloud my judgment. Abigail needed to see her father, but please don't hold that against her. The blame is entirely mine. I told her of the rules, but then chose to break them anyway."

Headrick looked like she was having none of it. "Be that as it may, Jane, that does not give you the right to overstep your role in our society and not go through the proper channels for requesting travel. This isn't like you at all and, unfortunately, it is also a markable offense."

Thomas nodded solemnly. "I understand, Councilor."

Mathias stepped forward, a look of pity on his face. "Angela, Thomas is young. I think we were all allowed a chance to make mistakes when we were starting out. I seem to recall a similar incident when you were heading up the Paris Headquarters."

Councilor Headrick looked infuriated. "How dare you, Benedict? We are not friends, nor would I say we are even acquaintances. I am your superior and you will treat me as such. And it's Councilor Headrick to you, regardless of how well we knew each other at one point." Headrick turned back to gaze on Thomas and I. "The two of you are to return to San Fransisco at once."

"Councilor," I began, "if you could just allow us a few more minutes with my father. I promise we will return within the hour." I felt that it was a reasonable request, but Headrick looked as if I had just asked to take over her position.

"Miss Jordan, you are not in a position to make any sort of

request. You were sent to San Francisco for a reason. To train. Whether or not you choose to do so is your choice, but you have no place here now." She extended her arm, pointing to the fireplace and the Time Line beyond. "Go."

I almost argued with her. This was my father, who I had not seen in almost a year. How could she dictate whether or not I could see him? But I didn't get the chance. Thomas placed his hand gently on my shoulder, and I knew what he was telling me to do. We needed to go, and we needed to go right now. I finally sighed and moved ahead to the Time Line. Thomas took no time at all in setting our location and we left the London Headquarters immediately, leaving Mathias to face the wrath of Headrick.

As soon as we returned to San Francisco, I told Thomas I needed to go find the pocket watch Bessie had given me. I promised him I would meet him wherever he'd like and he told me about a place called the Balboa Cafe on Fillmore Street. We agreed on meeting there. He seemed content with that and as I rode on a cable car back to my apartment, I continued to rewind and play again the memories in my head of what Sister Margaret had told us. The only thing that kept jumping to the front of my mind was the fact that my mother had not died on the bridge that night. I didn't know what to think or feel, and was secretly and perhaps guiltily glad my aunt had died and not my mother, but I brushed it off as the cable car came to a halt and I jumped off, walking the rest of the way to the Chambord Building.

When I unlocked the door and entered the apartment, I found it was empty. Bridget must still be at class and I assumed Ian was probably doing something at the Headquarters. I went straight to my room, opened the closet door, and pulled a shoebox from the highest shelf. I had placed anything valuable or meaningful from London in this box, and the first thing I saw when I opened it, was Phillip's letter. Everything he had said in the letter came flying back to me at once. *Life goes on…you will find someone…keep going.*

Had I been living my life to his requests? I had chosen to keep going, but had I tried to continue on with my life? Recently I had, but in our initial months in San Francisco I had allowed myself to be consumed by my thoughts. I had allowed these voices, or at least my telepathic sister, to torment me. Why did she want to torment me? Why did she want to cause me distress? What could have possibly happened to her that she would want me to feel as if I had killed those I had loved?

I brushed aside the thoughts and moved the letter to the side, but there was no pocket watch. There were a couple of things that had belonged to my mother and a few things from my father, but nothing else. Where was the pocket watch? I had put it in here; there was no doubt about it. I remembered when I packed everything before we left London. It had been in here. And now it wasn't.

My attention was suddenly drawn to my open door, to the door to Ian's room, directly across the hall from mine. Surely not. I took a deep breath and stood up, slowly making my way out of my room and to Ian's door, placing my hand on the doorknob. When I attempted to turn it however, the knob barely turned. It was locked. Why would he lock his bedroom door? I jiggled the handle again, as if it would suddenly come unlocked, but there was no success.

I sighed and went back to my room to get dressed for my date with Thomas, trying to convince myself I was overreacting. Why would Ian take the pocket watch that Bessie had given me? How would he even know about it? I had never said anything about it to him, at least not to my knowledge. The only way he would know about it was if he knew Bessie.

"No," I said out loud. "Stop this. You're overreacting." But was I?

Regardless of whether I was overreaching or not, I walked to my door and immediately shut it, turning the lock so it was just me inside the room, even though there was no one in the apartment with me. I began to get dressed, deciding to wear the same dress that I had worn the night I had first met Thomas. But as I did so, I no longer felt safe within my own apartment.

The Balboa Cafe wasn't anything over-the-top, but it was a great place to sit down and have a hamburger. As we waited for our food to arrive, Thomas and I mulled over the events of the day and I asked him his thoughts about Councilor Headrick.

"I'm with you on the idea that there is something there," Thomas responded. "However, we need to be careful. We don't want to tip her off on anything, and we also do not want her to be our enemy. I'm not saying she is working with anyone in particular, but whether she is or not, she is still heading up the Council and could do a lot of damage if that is what she wanted."

I nodded in response to this and then moved the subject of the conversation to Ian. "I tried to go into his room before I left tonight.

The door was locked. It's something I've never noticed before, but it definitely struck me as odd. The only reason I could come up with for locking a door in your own home would be if you were intent on hiding something."

Thomas considered this. "Why were you snooping anyway?"

"My mother's pocket watch," I responded. "I went to get it and it wasn't where I left it, and I know I left it there. I'm sure of it. I got suspicious and decided to try Ian's room, but like I said, the door was locked."

Our food arrived and the smell of freshly-cooked hamburgers and french fries momentarily distracted me from the conversation at hand. I dug into my food, slicing the hamburger in half, and then taking a big bite. As I savored the hamburger, I looked up to see that Thomas wasn't eating. He was staring at me, or at least he was looking at me, but it looked more like he was lost in his own thoughts. Finally, he spoke.

"We have to find out what this prophecy is about. Without it, we are just running around blind and we have no idea what the plan is, nor who is involved."

I swallowed my food and then responded. "You're right, but let's forget about it for a bit. It's best not to let yourself be consumed by these thoughts. Try your burger, I bet it's as delicious as mine."

He smirked at me. "Since when did you become such a wise one?" He picked up his burger and took a bite. I knew he enjoyed it as soon as he sat back and closed his eyes, swallowing his food.

"I've always been wise," I responded. "Now, shut up and keep eating."

He did as he was asked.

When we finally left the Balboa Cafe, night had fallen upon the city. I looked to Thomas to say our goodbyes, but his expression told me the night was just beginning for him.

"Surely you aren't leaving yet?" he asked me.

"I was going to," I responded. "Unless there is something else you had in mind?"

"Can I take you somewhere?"

I hesitated before responding. The fact that I had pushed myself to come on this date, and that we had made it through dinner without any interruptions from my subconscious, or my sister as I still hadn't completely determined who was responsible for what when it came to the thoughts in my head, was quite remarkable. I wasn't sure if I wanted to chance anything more, but at the same time I wasn't ready to go home just yet. When I got home, Ian would be there and I didn't know if I could deal with him at the moment.

"Where did you have in mind?" I finally asked.

"It's a surprise." He held out his hand. "Do you trust me?"

There was that word again. In the last year, I had put my trust into so many people and been betrayed that it was a very scary thought to do it again. But I did and I wondered if I always would. Everyone has at least one weakness. I took Thomas' hand and he smiled, pulling me along behind him to a motorbike parked alongside the road.

I looked at him in surprise. "Is this yours?"

"It sure is." He handed me a helmet and I took it. Considering I'd almost fallen off the Tower Bridge, I probably shouldn't fear a motorbike. Thomas put on a helmet as well and swung his right leg over and onto the other side of the bike. "Get on behind me."

I did as he asked. We sat there for a few moments before he finally said, "You need to put your arms around my waist if you don't want to go flying off."

I moved my arms and as I began to place them on his waist, I hesitated. I hadn't touched another man this intimately since Phillip. I immediately withdrew my hands.

"Are you alright?" Thomas asked. "We don't have to do this if you're uncomfortable."

I shook my head. "No, sorry. I mean, I'm fine. It's fine."

I took a deep breath and placed my arms around his waist, leaning into him. He started up the engine and before I could say or do anything more, we were pulling out into the road and racing down the streets of San Francisco. Even though I was wearing a helmet, my hair fell out the back and was blowing around my face. The breeze felt cool and refreshing against my cheeks. I felt exhilarated. Thomas drove for a while, taking us to the edge of the city towards the Golden Gate Bridge. He finally stopped the bike and parked just outside Fort Point, which was almost directly under the bridge.

We got off and walked down a ways until we were at the edge of the water. Thomas plopped himself down and laid on his back, looking up at the bridge and the stars. I hesitated again, briefly, and then lay down beside him, leaving enough distance between the two of us, of course.

"It's beautiful," Thomas said. "I love coming here and allowing my thoughts to come and go. It's a great place to come and reflect. I suppose you have places like that in London?"

I considered that for a moment. "I suppose yes. Towards the end of my time there I went up to Big Ben for a little bit and looked out at the city. But in the end, I only saw a war zone. Being here, in America, I feel like I can escape it all. Yes, I know there is a war going on, but I'm not constantly reminded of it. I'm not spending the majority of my nights, when I should be sleeping, in a bunker hoping my house will still be there the next morning."

Thomas leaned on his side to look at me and I did the same. He stared at me for a moment longer before saying, "I'm sorry about everything that has happened to you. I know what it's like to lose a mother, but like I said, for me it was slow and gradual. I can't even imagine losing so many people, and all at once. I wish I could take it away for you."

"I thought you said you didn't know your mother."

He smiled. "I should've been more specific. I didn't know my birth mother. After she left, my father remarried and the woman he married raised me as her own. A few years ago, she got sick and her life ended rather quickly."

"I guess we are kind of similar," I responded. "Both of us never knew our birth mother."

I wanted to say something more, but I had nothing. I only attempted a half-smile as a tear rolled down my cheek at the same time. Thomas extended his arm and wiped the tear away with his finger.

"Abby," he finally said, "there's something about you that makes me want to be a better person. I've always had careless, meaningless relationships with other girls, but with you I want something more. I used to go out with a different girl almost every night, and lot of the time I felt like I was using them, even though they always knew how I felt, and usually felt the same. Ever since I met you at that club, though, I haven't been out with another girl."

Thomas and I had known each other a couple months now, and he was now telling me he hadn't been out with anyone, except for me? This man was falling for me, and I knew I was falling for him. But there was a part of me resisting as well. That part that didn't want to let Phillip go. But then again, I wasn't sure if I ever wanted to let Phillip go completely. He had been an important part of my life. The things we'd done together, seen together, and laughed about together had all contributed to the person I was today. And I didn't want to change that.

I leaned into Thomas because I wanted to be with him. His lips were mere centimeters from mine. My eyes were closing. My breath was becoming ragged.

What are you doing? What about Phillip?

It was her voice again. Melanie. She was taunting me. It had to be her. She wanted me to feel guilty for being with Thomas, but why? What had I done to her? Why did she want me to feel this way? I crawled away from Thomas and stood up, bringing my hands to cover my face as I cried out.

"Abby!" It was Thomas' voice. His arms were around me, holding me to him. "Are you okay?"

I immediately pushed him away and took a step back. "I'm sorry,

Thomas. I can't do this. I just can't. Will you take me home? Please?"

He looked hurt. He thought it was him, but it wasn't. I knew that I could probably explain what had just happened, but even though it was something I had told him about before, it stay made me feel vulnerable. I just needed to be taken away from here, away from him, for the time being. He nodded and we went back to the bike. I put on the helmet he had given me earlier and climbed on behind him. I didn't want to, but I placed my arms around his waist, but not as tight this time. The engine of the bike came to life and we sped off again into the night, neither of us speaking a word.

CHAPTER TWELVE

Thomas dropped me off at the doorstep of the Chambord Building. I muttered a quick goodbye, not even looking at him, and then quickly made my way up to my apartment. I felt embarrassed, upset, and confused. I thought I had gotten over these thoughts. Phillip wanted me to move on with my life. He had said so in the letter he had left for me. Why was I still letting myself think he would want anything less of me? The worst part of it all was that I still didn't know whether or not these feelings were my own or if they had some sort of connection to my sister that I knew was out there somewhere.

"Why are you doing this to me?"

I didn't mean to ask it aloud, but I did. I said it to the empty space of the hallway as I made my way toward the door to my apartment. And for the first time in a long time, I got a response that sounded just like me. Although I knew who it really was this time.

I'm not doing anything. Those feelings are your own. I simply want for us to meet, now that you know about my existence.

I reached into my pocket, trying to find my keys. As I did, I carefully considered what I should say next and I knew there was no need to say it out loud. I didn't need anyone else seeing me do that. It would be even more proof for Ian to bring back Dr. Aldridge.

And what if I don't want to meet you? I asked her in my head. *Our mother clearly didn't want us to be together.*

And how do you know that?

The answer was I didn't know. A jingle. Finally, I had found my keys. I took them out and placed the key to the apartment in the deadbolt, turning it, all the while continuing to think about my answer.

If she had wanted us to be together, she wouldn't have separated us.

Again, how do you know that she separated us?

Logically, I guess that made sense. I knew Bessie had been my mother's mid-wife and there had been some sort of struggle on the night of my birth. Perhaps, in an effort to save us, my mother had only been able to grab me? What had she done with my sister? Had she even been able to get us both out of there? Had my aunt, before meeting her untimely death on the Tower Bridge, been able to hide my sister away somewhere?

I don't know if she did that. I just know she didn't want me to be a part of this world. She didn't want me to find out about any of this. If you aren't the one sending me these terrible thoughts I've been thinking and seeing, then where do they come from?

It all has to do with you. I'm just the voice of reason here.

She wasn't making any sense. *Why didn't you say something more before? Why didn't you say something like, "Hello, Abigail. This is your twin sister?"*

It wasn't time for you to know. I'll lead you to me when it's time. Goodbye.

And before I could say anything more, I knew she was gone. It was like she left the room, even though there was no room to leave.

Maybe she went to sleep? I had no idea, and it was then I realized I was still standing at the door to my apartment, one hand on the knob, and the other still on the key having just turned the deadbolt. I quickly turned the knob and entered the apartment, closing the door behind me.

I found Bridget awake, reading a book on the couch in our living area. She looked up at me over her reading glasses and smiled.

"You were out late? Date night?"

I nodded as I shrugged off my coat and hung it on the coatrack. Looking back at Bridget, I saw a look of surprise on her face as she turned back to her book. She had been joking when asking the question.

"I just went out to dinner with Thomas," I added hastily, trying to make it sound as if it wasn't anything special. I didn't know why I felt like I needed to justify it. It was as if I thought she too would make me feel guilty about going on a date with someone, even though it was what Phillip would have wanted.

"I'm happy for you," she finally replied, flicking her gaze up from her book and then back down again.

The thing was, she didn't look happy. I walked over to her and sat down next to her. When she didn't put the book down, I cleared my throat rather noticeably and she finally sighed and put the book to the side, looking up at me as she did.

"Are you okay?" I asked her. "We haven't really talked lately. I know I've been out and about, getting reacquainted I guess, but I feel as if you are distancing yourself from me. Remember when we had lunch? You mentioned that there was something you wanted to tell me."

Bridget bit her lip and looked away, taking off her reading glasses as she did. She immediately stood up, placed the glasses on the table, and walked into the kitchen. I heard the clank and clatter of the dishes as she began to wash them in the kitchen sink. I sighed, wondering if I should let this go, but decided against it, stood up, and walked into the kitchen.

"Bridget, please," I said. "Please, tell me what it is. Is there something going on with Ian I should know about?"

Bridget let out a long sigh as she placed the plate she was washing back into the sink and turned around, leaning against the counter, her hands covered in suds. She looked at me for a second, shook her head, and then turned around, grabbing a towel as she did and drying off her hands.

"I can't talk about this right now, Abigail."

Abigail. Very rarely had Bridget ever called me Abigail, even when she was mad at me. I realized I should probably let this issue rest and retire for the night, but I wanted her to know I was there for her.

"Remember, you can talk to me. I'm here for you. Okay?"

A stifled sob and then she said, "I know."

I wanted to walk to her and comfort her, but I knew there was some kind of internal battle she was trying to sort out for herself right now, and I needed to let her do that. And so I did.

The next day, I did my best to avoid Thomas. It wasn't difficult as he never came by the office. I simply sat in silence and worked on balancing the library's budget as well as making sure all necessary bills were taken care of. It was around noon, when I was planning to leave for lunch, that there was a knock at the office door and before I had to time process whether or not it might be Thomas, the door opened and a man stepped in. Thankfully, the man wasn't Thomas. He was of a similar height, and they looked to be about the same age, but his vibrant, fiery hair, as well as the freckles that dotted his face, set him apart from Thomas quite a bit.

As soon as he was in the room, he looked at me, and then he looked around the room in confusion, before looking back at me.

"My apologies," he finally said. "I was looking for Thomas Jane."

"He isn't here today," I finally said, and then stood up, remembering my manners, and held out my hand. "I'm Abigail Jordan. He hired me a few months ago to be his assistant."

The man laughed at this and held out his hand, taking mine. We shook briefly before he pulled away.

"Leave it up to Thomas to need an assistant," the man said. "I'm Oliver. Oliver Caldwell. Thomas and I are old friends." He then looked at his watch in confusion and looked back at me. "He's usually here this time of day, but I guess since he has an assistant now, that isn't the case. My only guess is he is dealing with the family business."

Family business. I got the impression that Oliver knew about Timekeeping, but he didn't want to say so in case I didn't know about Timekeeping. But, likewise, I didn't want to say anything in case he didn't know about Timekeeping. It was an awkward situation all the way around. There was a creak, and I looked up to see Alma standing in the doorway. Oliver turned around and saw her, and I saw something light up in his face. It was a quick flash, and then it was gone.

"Abigail," Alma said, looking away from Oliver, a slight blush on her cheeks, "Thomas sent me to tell you he wouldn't be in today and was wondering if you could finalize the list of donors for the library's upcoming charity event?"

Thomas wasn't coming in. Was he avoiding me? I wasn't sure why this mattered to me, as I was clearly doing the same thing to him. But it did.

"Of course," I finally said. "I was just about to head out for something to eat, but I will get that taken care of."

Oliver cleared his throat. "I don't mean to butt in, but would you two ladies like to come to lunch with me? I was going to go with Thomas, but he clearly isn't here, and I'm starving, to be quite honest."

Alma looked from Oliver to me, not knowing what to say.

"I guess I could do that," I finally said.

I looked over to Alma and she shrugged her shoulders and then nodded. And just like that, I was off to lunch with two people I barely knew. There I was being completely trusting again, but perhaps that was something that would always be my downfall.

Oliver took us to the Balboa Cafe, insisting it was his favorite place in the entire city. I wondered if this was some sort of sign, considering I had just been there yesterday with Thomas on the date that ended terribly. I decided not to protest, however. In a way, I felt like it kind of told me a little more about Thomas. Perhaps the Balboa Cafe was some kind of favorite pastime of his from living in San Francisco.

Perhaps, he was pretty close with Oliver, and the two of them would often come here when they were younger. I could envision them as young teenagers, bringing their first dates here on the night of a school dance. I smiled at that and let myself drift away into my thoughts.

"Miss Jordan."

I snapped out of my reverie and saw that Oliver was trying to get my attention.

"I'm sorry," I suddenly said. "I let myself be taken away for a moment. What were you saying? And please, call me Abigail."

"Oliver was asking how long you've been in America," Alma supplied.

"Oh," I said, "almost eight months."

Oliver nodded and looked away for a moment. I was getting the impression he and Alma knew each other a bit. I decided I might as well ask.

"So, do you two know each other?"

Oliver looked at Alma with an expression that almost looked as if he wasn't sure he should answer. It was the same expression he had worn earlier when he had referred to Thomas' *family business.*

"She's a Timekeeper," Alma whispered, and Oliver nodded in understanding.

I looked from Oliver to Alma. "So, he knows about Timekeeping."

Oliver answered. "Yes, but only because Thomas told me when we were younger, much to the dissatisfaction of his father. Although I'm beginning to think that most Timekeeper's share the information with their closest friends; I mean how could you not? It would be as if you were living a lie for almost your entire life."

I knew the feeling. I hadn't shared this information with my closest friend at first and it had almost ripped us apart. I truly believed there was no reason she shouldn't know. And she hadn't told anyone about it. She hadn't shared the information around. And who would believe her without proof? I secretly suspected the Council knew this, and this was why they weren't as stern on enforcing this particular rule. Instead they focused more of their time on who used their resources, such as the Time Line, illegally. It almost felt hypocritical of them to be upset with Thomas and I for traveling without permission, when my family started it all. I suddenly felt like that was power talking through me though, and I didn't like that feeling.

"In regards to your question though," Alma said, "Thomas introduced me to Oliver when I started my training."

"What's your story?" I asked her. "I don't know much about you, and I'd like to."

Alma smiled at that, but before she could answer, a waiter came to the table. I expected him to ask us for our drink orders, but what he actually said sent a cold shiver down my spine. He looked directly at Alma.

"Miss," he said, "I'm sorry, but we have a few customers uncomfortable with your presence here, and we need to ask you to leave."

Alma nodded, placed the napkin she had in her lap on the table, stood up, and walked out of the restaurant.

I looked back at the waiter. "I'm sorry, but what exactly is the problem?"

"Her kind isn't welcome in this type of establishment," an older woman at a nearby booth spat at me. "And you should be ashamed of yourself for associating with her. She knows where she belongs."

Oliver stood up. "Let's go, Abigail."

I looked between Oliver, the waiter, and the old woman. All of them continued to stare at me, and finally I stood up and walked out of the restaurant.

Alma was standing just outside the cafe, taking a puff on a cigarette. She looked up at us when we came out.

"My apologies guys. I just wasn't thinking. You two could have stayed though. Did you want to try somewhere else?" She took another puff on her cigarette, waiting for my response.

I looked at her in confusion, and then turned to Oliver who was rubbing his hand through his fiery hair.

I turned back to Alma. "I'm so confused. What just happened?"

"There are some places I can't go," Alma replied.

"But, why?"

Alma looked surprised. "Uh, because I'm black. Don't you have any places where colored people can't go where you're from?"

I thought about it, continuing to be appalled by the entire situation. "I mean, no. I don't think so. I guess I don't really know. Honestly, I've never gotten to know someone like—" I stopped myself.

A cheeky grin appeared on Alma's face. "Someone like me?"

I shook my head. "I'm sorry, I didn't mean it that way. I just—"

"It's fine," Alma cut me off. "Really. What matters to me is that you don't care what people think of you when you are with me. You could have stayed in there. You could have not gotten lunch with me at all. But you did. That's what matters."

I continued to look at Alma and then to Oliver, and then back to Alma again. I just didn't know how to process this situation. It was like meeting Councilor Winston all over again. I remembered his comments about people that didn't live up to his image. I knew that Hitler was killing people who also didn't live up to his image. I had just never seen anything so hateful, so vile, and close up before. I had never seen it directed to a person I knew. And it scared me.

"I just feel like we need to talk about this," I said.

Alma stepped forward, placing a firm hand on my shoulder as she did. "Honestly, Abigail. There's nothing to talk about. I'm fine, you're fine. Let's just forget this happened and get some lunch. Okay?"

I nodded and the three of us made our way to another destination, but in my head I still wasn't satisfied. I could tell this wasn't anything new for Alma, and that she was simply moving on as she had probably done countless other times. But I felt like I needed to do more for her. And I wanted to try to accomplish that.

CHAPTER THIRTEEN

November 1944

Weeks passed and I heard nothing from my sister. The hallucinations had also stopped completely. The only thing that remained were the dreams. I was still constantly plagued by dreams of Phillip and my family dying around me. The only difference was I was used to it now. I was used to waking up the middle of the night in a cold sweat. I was used to flailing around in my bed sheets. Luckily, I had stopped drawing attention to myself. When I woke up in the darkness of my room, I knew it was just a dream. I no longer screamed. Bridget no longer needed to come into my room and comfort me.

Except for Alma, who had begun to come to the library regularly during the day for lunch, and Ian, of course, I had no contact with anyone from the Timekeeping world. Thomas had not been in the office for weeks now. He appeared to be giving me space, or perhaps I had scared him off. I had no idea. I was grateful Alma didn't pry, or ask what was going on between us. She simply came to be a friend. During the weeks that passed, as October slowly faded away into November, I began to learn more about Alma. I learned her father, Beauford James IV, came to San Francisco in the 1920s looking for work and had met and fallen in love with her mother, Meta Johnson. Her father worked for Hunters Point Naval Shipyard, while her mother came from a prominent Timekeeping family in Africa. Alma's mother had trained at the San Francisco Headquarters when she was Alma's age and had decided to stay on, working her way up to be one of the members on the San Francisco Council.

The Headquarter Councils were another thing I learned about the Timekeeping community. Apparently, every Timekeeping Headquarters had a Council that was similar to the Council that led the Timekeeping world. At the head of the Council at each Headquarters, was the head of the Headquarters, so in San Francisco's case, it was Thomas.

During all of this, I was constantly reminded of what had taken place at the Balboa Cafe. For Alma, I knew it was something that happened to her and she moved on, but it continued to haunt me. I couldn't fathom how people could be so cruel toward another human being. But then I remembered the likes of Bessie, and how she had destroyed my mother, or aunt, and I was reminded that's how some people were, unfortunately.

And then one day, Alma asked that I come to her ball. As I had not so long ago, Alma would have a Timekeeper's Ball in which she would be fully initiated into the society. I kept finding myself drawn into the world of the Timekeepers, no matter how much I tried to stay away. I was beginning to fully accept this was who I was, whether or not I actually liked it.

"The ball is this Saturday."

Alma and I were once again eating lunch in the office of the library. I looked over the calendar that Thomas kept on his desk and saw that this Saturday was November 18. I had nothing planned, so of course I would go. Before I could respond, however, the door to the office opened abruptly and Thomas stood in the doorframe. I was taken aback by his appearance. His normally clean-shaven face was replaced by a scraggly looking beard that he was clearly not maintaining. The dark bags under his eyes indicated he had not been sleeping and my heart suddenly beat faster. Had I caused this? Had I done this to him? I needed him to know, wanted him to know, that he wasn't the reason for my feelings. But I guess that wasn't true. Technically, he was the reason I was having these conflicted feelings, but he needed to understand it was me, not him.

"Abby," Thomas said. He looked from me to Alma, and then walked into the room and knelt in front of me. I leaned back in shock. Was he going to propose? But then I shook my head. Of course, he wasn't going to propose. How absurd could I possibly be?

Thomas took my hand and looked into my eyes. "It's Mathias."

That made my heart skip even faster. "What about Mathias?"

"Councilor Headrick has put out an injunction," Thomas began, "prohibiting Mathias from continuing in his position as head of the London Headquarters."

"Can she do that?" I asked.

"Yes," Thomas said, "and no. There are rules. However, she has power as head of the Council to issue a temporary injunction. She has twenty-four hours before the injunction is lifted. During that time, she has to prove to the Council that Mathias is inept at continuing in his position. There will be a hearing, during which evidence and testimony will be presented by Headrick, Mathias, and other parties. The Council will then vote on whether or not Mathias can continue in his position. The thing is, the injunction was issued yesterday."

"When is the hearing?" I asked, standing up.

"In thirty minutes," Thomas replied. "I only just found out. I think Headrick was trying to cover it up. Ian and I were going to go. Ian was going to provide testimony in support of Mathias's character and I thought you should have a chance to have your own voice on the matter. I've already gotten approval for us to travel to the hearing."

"Let's go," I said. I looked to Alma. "I'll see you later?"

Alma looked appalled at the idea. "Are you joking? I'm going with you. I may not be able to put my own two cents in, but I can offer moral support."

I smiled at that. I really did like Alma. Together, the three of us made our way down into the Headquarters so that we could travel to the hearing.

The hearing was to take place at the Central Headquarters. Thomas quickly found Ian and we went to the Time Line to travel. When we left the San Francisco Headquarters, the four of us were dry. Upon arriving at the Central Headquarters, we landed in a pool of water. It was as if I had been dropped into an ocean of water from high above. Below me was what looked like never-ending darkness. Above me, I could see the surface. I could see a ceiling and on that ceiling, I could see a clock. The clock had no hands, a common symbol in the

Timekeeping community to represent the idea that time itself is endless. I stayed like that for a moment, underneath the surface, looking up at the blurry image of the clock until finally a hand touched mine and I was being pulled to the surface.

I was surprised to find that as soon as I broke the surface, I was standing up. It was shallow water. But I had been underneath the surface. I had been dropped into what felt like the deep end of a pool. But now there was no deep end. Thomas stood directly in front of me, his hand still clasped in mine. He beckoned me forward and I stepped out of the pool of water onto concrete and I was immediately dry. It was as if a strange, heated wind suddenly came over my body and everything that had been dripping wet was now dry, as if it had never been wet at all.

"I don't understand," I said, looking behind me and back at the pool of water. It was then that I noticed we were in a room with multiple pools of water at various different points. Individuals were stepping out of these pools of water and onto the concrete just as we had.

"Central Headquarters has never made much sense," Thomas said. "I wouldn't try to dwell on it too much. The only thing to know is that water is often seen as an important concept that goes hand in hand with time. Timekeepers see time as a stream, just as water is a stream. They see it as being endless. Always constant."

I nodded, looking again at the pool of water we had just come out of. Thomas' hand was still clasped in mine, and I didn't pull away from it. He began to lead me down the concrete row, past all of the pools of water, Ian and Alma in tow. We stepped through a tall archway and into a well-lit hallway. Intricate designs of a clock were etched into the walls of the hallways as we made our way toward wherever the hearing was taking place.

"What country are we in?" Alma asked. "What city hosts the Central Headquarters?"

"Isn't that the question of the day," Thomas said. "Honest answer? No one knows. No one has ever been able to find a way out of Central Headquarters. The only way in and out is through the Time Line, or in this case, the pools of water. You have to have your pocket watch with you, of course. Once you travel to another Headquarters, you can go back to the mainland by using their exit. But as for the way in here, from land that is, no one knows. Not even Headrick. Many people have assumed that it was only known by the original Timekeeping family, but of course many still say that is a fairy tale."

Thomas gave me a look out of the corner of his eye, reminding me he believed my story. That I was an original Timekeeper. I had no idea what was going on. He didn't seem upset. He didn't seem mad at me. Maybe he hadn't been avoiding me at all? Maybe he had just been busy.

We eventually found our way into a large, square chamber with stands on both sides of the room. At the front of the room was a long table at which sat, I assumed, the Timekeeping Council. I recognized several faces from my ball, but there were some I didn't recognize as well. At the middle of the table sat Councilor Headrick, a stern expression on her face. She sat back quietly in her chair as she carefully observed each person who walked into the room. Her hair was pulled back so tightly in a bun it looked as if the skin on her face was being stretched. When she saw me, nothing changed on her face. There was no concern. She simply looked at me and then moved on to look at the other Timekeepers entering the chamber.

I followed Thomas to a table directly in front of the Council's table. Mathias sat waiting. When I was close enough, I broke away from Thomas's grasp on my hand and took a seat next to Mathias. A smile appeared on his face as I did. I took him all in. It had only been a few weeks since I had last seen him, but he had cleaned up nicely for his hearing. His hair was still long, but he had completely shaved off the beard that he had been growing out. He looked as if he had been getting some rest, so that was good. He leaned in and pulled me in for a hug. After a moment, he pulled away and looked at me again.

"You came," he said.

"Of course," I said. "We can't let them do this to you."

He smiled at that. There was a loud sound as Councilor Headrick beat a gavel. Thomas took a seat next to me, Alma next to him, and Ian at the end of the line. We all turned our attention to Headrick, who was now walking around from behind the table to address the chamber as a whole, her heels clicking angrily against the chamber floor. The sound reverberated off the walls, making it even louder than it really was. She wore a tight, black dress that covered her entire body, almost as if it was swallowing her up.

"Good afternoon," Councilor Headrick said, her voice echoing throughout the chamber. "We are here today to determine whether or not Timekeeper Mathias Benedict should continue in his duties as the head Timekeeper of the London Headquarters. In the past twenty-four hours, I have given out an injunction for Timekeeper Benedict to cease all Timekeeping-related activity. We shall hear evidence today and the Council will vote. The majority vote will determine whether or not Timekeeper Benedict shall continue in his role.

"I shall begin first by presenting my evidence to the Council. All opposed should wait until all evidence is presented before presenting any opposition against it. My first piece of evidence against Timekeeper Benedict is his unwillingness to delegate responsibilities to other Timekeepers in running the London Headquarters. Since Benedict has taken over for his father, he has assisted in the training of only two Timekeepers: his daughter, Abigail Jordan, and Ian Cross, both of whom are here today. Furthermore, Benedict has always opposed any outside help. As many of you know, the successful running of a Timekeeping Headquarters falls not only on its leader but also the Council that helps run the Headquarters, the individuals that conduct meetings with government officials, the individuals that keep a careful record of all events on the Timeline, and many more. The positions are endless. All of these tasks Benedict has taken on himself. And unfortunately, he hasn't been doing them well."

Councilor Headrick looked at Mathias, and then the room as a whole, before continuing.

"In regards to his attendance at annual trainings and ceremonies, well let's just say his attendance isn't even a factor. Benedict has attended no Timekeeper initiations, except those which were hosted at the London Headquarters. Benedict has not attended our annual trainings, at which all headquarter leaders get together. Overall, his participation in our society is lacking. This takes me into my next point; his lack of regard for our rules.

"Timekeepers have strict rules in place. We cannot allow individuals whom we are training to become compromised. This is something that Benedict allowed when he was training his daughter, Abigail. While it was Abigail's decision to almost save her fiancé from death, Benedict allowed it to happen. As her mentor, he should have intervened. He should have stopped her, even though she thankfully stopped herself. Furthermore, even after his daughter's reassignment by the Council, Benedict still allowed her to break our rules. While at the American Headquarters, Abigail took part in illegal, unsanctioned travel using the Time Line. While this was primarily Timekeeper Jane's offense, as a seasoned headquarters leader, Benedict should have immediately reported this illegal travel to his Headquarters. Instead, he went out on the town with Miss Jordan and Timekeeper Jane."

Headrick looked away from Mathias and turned on her heel to face the Council.

"Councilmen and women, I feel that this issue is cut and dry. Mathias Benedict has overstepped his boundaries on numerous occasions. He has allowed his judgment to be comprised. He has refused to fully participate in our customs and practices. He has been warned on numerous occasions to change his ways. He has been warned not only by myself, but also by my predecessor, Councilor Winston. I hope you will see this for what it is: a blatant disrespect for our community as a whole. Thank you."

Councilor Headrick went back to the Council's table and took her seat. She looked pretty satisfied with the information she had presented to the Council, and while I was still suspicious of her actions, I had to admit to myself everything she said was true. Next, we heard testimony from various Timekeepers who testified to the positive character of Mathias. We also heard negative feedback from other Timekeepers as well. And then the time came for us to present our testimony. Ian stood up first, and I took a deep breath. As much as he had been on my nerves lately, as much as he had upset me or acted suspiciously, I knew he would set this right. I knew he would tell the Council how Mathias had been a great mentor, a great leader.

Ian stood up and looked around the room. He looked at Mathias for a moment, and then turned his attention to the Council.

"Councilmen and women," Ian began, "many probably assume that I am here today to testify to the good, moral character of Mathias Benedict, who was my mentor and teacher for several years before I became his assistant. Unfortunately, I cannot do that."

The silence in the room was deafening. I stood up.

"Ian," I spat.

"Silence."

I looked up to Councilor Headrick who had stood up, a look of pure anger on her face. Her eyes shot daggers at me and I returned the look.

"You will take your seat," Headrick said, "or you will be removed."

A hand touched mine and I looked to see Mathias looking up at me. He gestured for me to sit, and I did. But as I did, I continued to give Headrick a look that told her I disagreed with everything she stood for.

Headrick took her seat and nodded at Ian to continue.

"Thank you, Councilor Headrick," Ian continued. "Ladies and gentlemen, during my time training with Mathias Benedict, I came to know a man who has shunned himself completely from society. He wants nothing to do with the outside world. And, even though she may speak of his good character now, there was a time when his daughter, Abigail Jordan, did not trust this man. She even went so far as to suggest he had killed her biological mother, Elisabeth Callaghan. While that has since proven not to be true, it goes to show how bitter Mathias Benedict has become. He has allowed himself to become a person no one can bring themselves to trust. And he has done that to himself.

"Furthermore, during my time with Abigail and her father, I saw little training being done. By the time Abigail came to the American Headquarters, her training was so sparse she knew very little of our customs and practices. I do not think Mathias Benedict is fit to continue running the London Headquarters, nor do I think he should be responsible for the training of any future Timekeepers. Thank you."

As Ian walked forward to take his seat, he whispered to me, "Your turn." A smug smile appeared on his face as he took his seat, and in that moment, I despised him. I wished I had never met him.

"Miss Jordan?"

I looked up to Headrick, her attention on me again. I stood up and began to address the Council.

"Ladies and gentlemen of the Council," I began, "I have to be honest with you. What you have heard today is all true. It may have been spoken in a way to shape a specific individual's narrative—" I directed my attention to Ian when I said this, and then continued "—but it was true. But that's only because in the prime of his life, my father, Mathias Benedict, lost everything. He lost his wife and his child. He lost his existence and he became a person who seemed cold or unloving, but this is far from the truth. Initially, yes, my father was cold-hearted to me. I didn't trust him. But after what happened to me last February, he became a father. He became someone I care about very much. He cares deeply about this world. And when he let me go that night, to save my fiancé, he did so not because he wanted to break the rules, but because he didn't want to take away my free will, which at the end of the day is something we are all supposed to value as Timekeepers, is it not? I was initially very skeptical about being a Timekeeper, but I could tell it was something he valued tremendously. Please, don't take that away from him. Thank you."

With that, I took my seat. Mathias took my head and I looked at him and smiled. He returned the smile, and we turned our attention back to the Council for their vote.

A woman at the end of the council's table stood up.

"All in favor of removing Mathias Benedict as the Head of the London Headquarters, raise your hand," the woman said.

Several hands went up.

"All opposed, please raise your hands," the woman continued.

In the end it was close, but it didn't matter. In the end, my father lost by one measly vote.

"Mathias Benedict," Councilor Headrick said, standing up, "the majority has voted that you will be removed from your role as Head of the London Headquarters. I am reassigning you to the Paris Headquarters in a role to be determined by Timekeeper Bouvier. You have twenty-four hours to vacate the London Headquarters." Headrick banged her gavel and everyone in the room began to leave.

I turned to Mathias, but he was still smiling.

"It's okay, Abigail," he said, pulling me in for another hug. "Maybe it's time for a change. Maybe this is a good thing."

"It's not fair," I said.

"It will be okay," Mathias said. "I promise. But I need to go clean out. I will talk to you soon. Okay?"

I nodded at him. "Okay."

Not even a second after we got back to the American Headquarters, I pushed Ian against the wall.

"How could you do that?" I spat at him. "He gave you everything."

He continued to smile. "You said it yourself, Abigail. Did I lie? I really don't think I did."

"Abby." Thomas put his hand on my shoulder.

"Thomas is right," Alma said. "He isn't worth getting worked up over."

I stepped away from Ian. "He trusted you. And you betrayed him." I turned on my heel and left them all behind me. I needed to get away from here.

I avoided Ian for the rest of the week. I went about my days doing the work that needed to be done, while in the back of my mind I continued to ruminate over everything I knew, everything I had learned. I had a twin. My mother might still be alive. Ian wasn't the person I thought he was. Mathias had been removed from his position. Bridget was going through something she wanted to tell me, needed to tell me, but didn't feel like she could. And then there was Thomas. The way that I was feeling about him. The date that we went on. Everything seemed so complicated that I was grateful for the distraction of Alma's Timekeeper's Ball. It would be a needed distraction from everything going on in my life.

On Saturday evening, I stood in front of a long mirror with Alma as she did my hair. She smiled at me in the mirror as she brought a comb down through my hair and began to pull it together into a bun. Someone at the Headquarters had taken my size and found a beautiful, sleeveless, cream-colored gown that fell to the floor and pooled to the ground around my feet. Alma herself wore a black gown that also fell to the floor, but was a bit different in that one side was sleeveless whereas the other side had a long sleeve that fell down her arm. She wore the dress gracefully.

"You look beautiful," Alma said to me.

I turned to her after she made the final adjustments to my hair.

"As do you," I said. "This is your night after all."

She beamed at me just as there was a knock at the door.

"Come in," Alma said.

The door opened and Thomas stepped in. He looked first to Alma, smiled at her, and complimented her dress. Then, his eyes moved to me and the emotions I saw in them were incomprehensible. Passion. Desire. Protection. He stood there, speechless, continuing to take me in. He wore a simple yet handsome black evening suit. His hair was combed, and he was clean-shaven. I could tell in that moment why he was such a hit with the ladies.

"Abigail," Thomas said, "you look, breathtaking."

"Gee, thanks, asshole."

We both turned to look at Alma in the middle of the room, a hand on her hip and throwing Thomas a sassy expression.

Thomas blushed. "I'm sorry."

Alma walked forward and pushed Thomas jokingly.

"I'm only joking with you, Jane," she said. "Lighten up."

As she walked out of the room, she muttered quietly, but still loud enough for us to hear, "You two are too cute," under her breath.

"Abby," Thomas said, "I was wondering, well I wasn't sure if maybe, um, I guess I wanted to know if—"

"Well, spit it out," I said to him.

"Can I escort you to this ball?"

A smile lit up my face. "Of course, you can, but what about Alma?"

"It's tradition for the parents to escort their child in."

I guess that made sense. Technically, when Mathias had done so, he had been both my parent and my teacher.

"Very well," I said.

Thomas walked over to me and held out his arm. I placed my arm in his and we began walking from the spare bedroom to the ballroom, which I had yet to lay eyes on.

Thomas led me down the hallway of the guest rooms and

through the library. Several people were coming in off the hallway that led to the Time Line, obviously traveling in from other Timekeeping locations. Thomas led me through a door at the other end of the library and into another narrow hallway. At the end of the hallway stood two large, double doors that were wide open. Beyond I could see glints of gold and glass. Music was pouring from the room as well as the chatter of those that had already arrived. As we walked through the double doors, I almost stopped breathing at how breathtaking the room was.

Thomas and I stood at the top of a large staircase. The ballroom itself was two floors, the upper floor circled around the lower floor. Tables and chairs were positioned on the upper floor for dining, so guests would descend to the lower level for dancing, and, I assumed, the initiation ceremony, as there was a stage erected at the far end of the room, directly in front of a large clock made entirely out of glass. The upper floor also allowed onlookers to gather by the rails and look out over the scene below, which many couples were currently doing, gazing down at the Timekeepers that were already dancing.

"Shall we?"

I looked over to Thomas who was gazing down at the lower level.

"Sure," I said, "but don't give me any grief about my dancing."

"Likewise."

We kept our arms linked as we descended the steps. I wanted to freeze this moment, to make it permanent. In this moment, I could imagine no problems awaited me in the world outside. There was no prophecy that needed to be unraveled. There were no nefarious villains out to get me. There were no individuals constantly betraying my trust. There was no war, no death. It was a nice thought, but it was only that, a thought.

As soon as we stepped onto the ballroom floor, Thomas pulled me along and I was immediately swaying rhythmically throughout the room with him. My heart began to beat faster, and I couldn't help but imagine what it would have been like to dance like this with Phillip on our wedding night. We had never gotten that far. We had never been able to practice dancing for that particular occasion.

"A penny for your thoughts?" Thomas asked.

I looked into his eyes. Everything about him was so familiar, yet so new at the same time. A part of me felt like I had known him longer than I actually had.

"I'm sorry about the date," I said.

It wasn't what I had meant to say. I had considered telling him that he looked nice, or that I was even more untrusting of Ian, or that it was unfair what had happened to Mathias earlier in the week. But I didn't want to say any of that. I knew if I was going to get anywhere in the world, if I was going to go forward, I needed to let people know about my problems once in a while. And while all of those other things were genuine problems, there was also this relationship that was blooming around it. And I wanted this relationship. I needed it.

"Don't be sorry," Thomas said softly. "You've been through a lot. You're still going through a lot."

"You avoided me after that, though."

Thomas sighed. "I only wanted to give you some space. I didn't want to push you. This is something you have to figure out on your own. Obviously, if you need to talk about it, I'm here for you, but I didn't want to be intrusive."

He began to twirl me. It caught me off guard, but I quickly let myself be taken into it, allowing him to bring my hand up over my head, and allowing my body to spin around. I laughed as I came back to stand in front of him, and fell into him a little at the same time.

And then I saw him. He was standing at the other end of the room, but I was looking right at him, clear as day. *Elijah.*

Thomas looked in the same direction. "What is it?"

"It's him," I said. "It's Elijah."

I stepped away from Thomas and made my way toward Elijah. I knew Thomas was following and as we got closer, Elijah stepped away from the ball and made his way through a side door and into the hallway beyond. When Thomas and I stepped through the door, he was standing there waiting for us.

"Why do you only show up at balls?" I asked him as soon as we had stepped through the door and Thomas had closed it behind him.

Elijah smiled at this. "It's the perfect place. Not everyone here knows each other. It allows me to easily communicate with you without it being odd. It's just casual conversation."

"Unless someone saw us coming in here," I replied. "But anyway, you didn't tell me before, but you're my uncle, aren't you?"

"I have to admit, Abigail," Elijah responded, "when you're in a tight situation, your ability to uncover the facts is truly remarkable."

"Have you been keeping tabs on me?" I asked.

Elijah raised an eyebrow and then replied, "I have my sources."

Thomas cleared his throat. "I don't mean to be rude, but we

should probably get to the facts as quickly as possible. Someone is bound to notice us missing, and I do need to be present for Alma's initiation, being her mentor and all."

"Of course," Elijah responded.

"Well," I said, "I think the most important thing is to find out what this prophecy entails."

Elijah looked uncomfortable at that statement and I had a sudden jolt in my gut as I thought about why.

"You don't know, do you?"

Elijah shook his head. "I'm sorry, Abigail. If I had known, I would have made sure to tell you the night we first met. Your mother, my sister, was a very secretive woman who was bound to protecting you. In doing that, she only trusted in me the bare minimum. She thought it might put me in danger to know the full extent of it all, and obviously, she had planned for things to go much differently."

"Well," I said, "I need you to at least tell me everything you do know. I need to know if my mother is alive. I need to know if my aunt is alive. I need to know who to be on the lookout for. Did you even know my mother supposedly had twins? I need to know something. Anything."

"I didn't know about the twins," Elijah answered, "but I did know about their plot to switch places that night. Eleanor is dead. She died on the bridge that night. As for your mother, I have not had any contact with her since that night. It was the perfect scenario for her, as Eleanor had broken away from our family years prior. She ceased all contact with our family, so for your mother to assume her place, would be the perfect way to hide herself from the Timekeeping world."

"Do you think she knows?" I asked him. "Do you think she knows everything is falling apart? Do you have any kind of powers with her?" I told him what we had found out about telepathy.

"Your mother and Eleanor had that power," Elijah confirmed, "but I did not. They were identical twins, whereas I was a fraternal twin. I was never supposed to be born, at least that is what my mother always said. She even hinted that she had considered drowning me shortly after my birth, but she thought she might keep me around for later use."

I was taken aback at what he was saying. He was talking about my grandmother, and from what he was saying, she sounded like the exact opposite of anyone I'd ever want to meet. She sounded like Bessie.

"Did my mother tell you anything else?" I asked. "Did she give you any other instructions when you spoke with her?"

Elijah shook his head again. "Your mother told me nothing else. However, there is more you need to know about my family. We are not good people, Abigail. Our mother, she is the exact opposite of what a mother should be. And I know she is behind this. She knows you exist, and she will stop at nothing—"

The door to the hallway opened and Councilor Headrick appeared in the doorway.

"Jane," she said, "I've been looking for you. We are about to begin the initiation ceremony."

She looked beyond Thomas at Elijah.

"And who is this?"

"Matthew Conway," Elijah said, his British accent suddenly replaced with an American one. "I'm one of the historians here at the American Headquarters."

"And do you have your invitation, Mr. Conway?" Headrick asked.

"I'm afraid not," Elijah responded, "I assumed all who worked at the Headquarters were invited."

"Unfortunately not," Headrick responded. "Only those with invitations may attend the balls. Please return to your post and resume your duties. Jane. Jordan. Follow me."

Thomas and Headrick began to walk out of the hallway, but I hesitated, remaining where I stood. Headrick, sensing that I wasn't following, turned around and raised an eyebrow.

"Jordan," Headrick said, "the initiation is about to begin."

"Yes," I responded, "but I was wondering if I could speak with Mr. Conway a moment longer?"

Headrick stepped forward, stopping a mere inch from my face. I could feel the warmth of breath as she spoke.

"Again, Jordan," she said, "you seem to lack the understanding of when an order is given. Now, go."

I did as I was told, not knowing when, or even if, I'd have the chance to see Elijah again.

The rest of the evening took place as it had at my own ball, with the exception of a public, violent murder of a Timekeeping official, of course. Alma was called up to the stage and Headrick initiated her into the world of Timekeeping with Thomas and her parents by her side. She received her very own pocket watch, and she became a fully initiated Timekeeper. Afterwards, dancing commenced again. It was interesting to see the aftermath of the ceremony as I had obviously not been conscious for the rest of my own.

After speaking with Alma and her family, Thomas broke away and was now walking toward me. He seemed intent on getting to me and would not allow anyone to distract him. One person even stopped him to engage in conversation, but he said something to them and then continued on his trek toward me. When he reached me, he held out his hand, which I took, and we were dancing again.

I leaned in close to him and put my arms around his neck, placing my head against his shoulder.

"Is it wrong that I have feelings for you, but also for Phillip?" I asked.

"No," he responded. "In fact, I think I would be a little worried if you didn't have those feelings. I think that's what makes you human."

I lifted my head and looked into his eyes. They were eyes I could get lost in. They were eyes I could trust. I wondered, if maybe I took the time to fully look into a person's eyes, if I could see from the get-go whether it would be worth it to trust them. Worth it to begin a relationship with them.

"I think I'm falling for you, Thomas Jane."

He grinned. "And I think I'm falling for you, Abigail Jordan. I've never felt like this. I've never wanted this. Not until I met you."

I rested my head against his chest, his arm holding me around my waist, pulling me close to him.

"I wish it could be like this forever," I said. "I wish this moment could last forever. In the last year, everything in my life has changed. And I have a strong feeling it's all about to change again."

We danced like that for a while. Him holding me. Me holding him. But what finally broke us apart was when I saw Ian. He was at the other end of the ballroom, in a corner. And he was talking to Headrick.

"Thomas," I said. "Ian and Headrick seem to be having quite the conversation."

Thomas let go of me, turned around, and looked to where I had gestured.

"I still can't believe what he said about Mathias," I said. "Mathias trusted him. He didn't deserve what Ian did to him."

I didn't trust Ian. I couldn't. And then I remembered his locked bedroom, and I wondered what was in there that he didn't want people to see. Tonight might be the only time I could get in there while he was away. I pondered the idea for a moment, and then decided I would give it a try.

"Thomas, I need to go home and do a few things."

Thomas looked back at me, raising his eyebrows.

"What are you thinking?" he asked.

"I'm thinking I'm ready for some answers."

"Abby, please be careful with whatever it is you are planning to do."

I nodded. "I will be."

I was done playing games. Ian wasn't who I thought he was, and it was time I proved it. Once at the Chambord Building, I made my way up to our apartment, unlocking the door and slamming it behind me, locking it as I did. I made my way to Ian's bedroom door and jiggled the handle. It was still locked, but I knew I could get around that. I found a bobby pin in my room and twisted it, turning it into a key that I would use to unlock the door. After only a moment or two, I had the door unlocked and Ian's room was before me. I shut the door behind me.

His room was surprisingly tidy. His bed was made, and there really wasn't much in the way of personal possessions. I went straight to his closet, and upon opening the door, I found all of his clothes, hanging neatly, and at the bottom, a shoebox. Kneeling down to the floor, I lifted the lid off of the shoebox.

Inside the shoebox were letters. The letters I had left for Ian to mail Mathias, tucked carefully inside. But that wasn't it. In addition to my letters, there were unopened letters from Mathias as well. I also found the pocket watch Bessie had given me, the one I now assumed was my aunt's. I quickly pocketed it.

A clicking sound came from the door to Ian's room and then the door opened. Before I could stand up, before I could defend myself, before I could even move away from the box, Ian was running into the room and dragging me by my hair across the floor. I cried out in pain. It felt like he was going to pull the hair out of my head. After he had dragged me away from the box, he picked me up and threw me on the bed. I began to push myself up, screaming as I did, but he was on top of me before I could get up any further, his mouth inches away from mine. I closed my eyes, hoping he would stop, continuing to scream for help, until he clasped his hand down over my mouth, muffling my screams. Because he was so close to my face, I could smell his breath, his dinner. It sent chills down my body. He grabbed my face and forced me to look at him, but I kept my eyes closed. At least I tried to until he used his other hand to pry my eyelids open so that I could see him. The force of his body on top of mine was keeping me pinned to the bed.

"Oh, the things I'd like to do to you," he said, smiling. "Unfortunately, I have eyes only for your sister, and despite my ulterior motives, I am a faithful man." He reached ahead of me and grabbed one of his pillows, taking off the pillowcase, and then he flipped me over and tied my hands. His strength continued to keep me pinned to the bed, and even if it hadn't, I honestly wondered if I would be able to do anything more anyway. I felt frozen, almost outside of my body. And my mind was racing because he had mentioned my sister. I was right all along. He did know her. He had thought I was her that day in the library. He used another pillowcase to tie up my feet as well. He finally climbed off the bed to observe his work; that smug smile that had been painted on his face earlier was still there as he looked down at me.

"Go ahead and scream again if you want," Ian said. "It will fit my *narrative* as you called it. I will be calling Bridget in a bit, telling her how you've lost your mind, how you made a mess of our kitchen by throwing things at the walls, and how I had to restrain you. And then we will call Aldridge and have you taken away."

Ian stepped forward and gripped my hair again, pulling me off of the bed and out into the hallway. I screamed in pain but Ian didn't care as he pulled me down the hall, knocking my body into the walls as he did. He jerked me into the living room, and then into the kitchen, leaving me in the middle of the floor. He threw open cabinets and began throwing plates against the wall. They smashed into thousands of pieces.

"Wise plan," Ian said, "leaving the ball early. Hoping to avoid me, and coming back here to sneak into my room. Unfortunately for you, I've always been pretty perceptive. You can't throw me off, Abigail. I've always been, and will always be, two steps ahead. Every. Single. Time."

I didn't respond.

He looked at me for a moment and then smiled again. "You didn't think I would hurt you, did you? You had your suspicions about me, but you honestly believed I wouldn't hurt you. Damn, Abigail. You really are too trusting."

Ian walked over to the phone and began dialing. I assumed he was calling Bridget at work. She didn't have class today.

"Hey, Bridge," Ian said.

"Don't listen to him," I shouted. "He's lying."

"Yeah," he said, "she's freaking out. She's throwing things against the wall. Please come home. I don't know what to do."

I continued to scream and scream, but Ian hung up the phone and made his way toward the cabinet, opening it up and pulling out an unmarked bottle.

"Perhaps you'd like some tea?" he asked me.

He opened the bottle and then reached into his pocket and pulled out a syringe.

"I think we're out though," he continued. "But this will do just fine. It's my secret ingredient."

And then it hit me. He'd been drugging me the entire time. He was putting whatever was in the container in my tea. I thought back to all of my hallucinations, every time I saw something that wasn't there. Every time, I had had tea. And Ian had made me the tea.

"It was you," I said. "You've caused the hallucinations. Why are you doing this?"

"To finish what Bessie started," he said, stepping toward me with the syringe. I began to push away from him, but he fell quickly to his knees and plunged the syringe into my neck.

Immediately, everything started to become blurry and disjointed. I was conscious of the fact that Ian had untied me. And then I began to see things. I was in the kitchen, but there was water? I looked up to the ceiling and could see the Tower Bridge above me.

A door was opening.

"Where is she?"

Bessie appeared before me and I lunged forward, putting my hands around her neck and pushing her to the ground.

"I hate you!" I shouted at her. I began to choke the breath out of Bessie, waiting until I could see the whites of her eyes. And then there was a searing pain at the side of my head, and everything went dark.

CHAPTER FOURTEEN

My mother stood before me. The two of us stood on the Golden Gate Bridge, her arm extended out toward me. As she had in my previous dreams, she wore that same white dress that blew in the wind with her hair.

"Abigail."

"I don't know what to do," I told her. "Are you still alive? Are you out there? I have no idea how to stop any of them. What do I do?"

She continued to extend her arm out in front of her, reaching for me, but she couldn't reach me.

"Abigail," she said, "they are closing in. Be careful."

And then waves from the San Francisco Bay roared up and over the bridge and my mother disappeared beneath them.

There was still darkness, but there was also a searing pain at the side of my head. It felt as if someone had hit me with something large, something metal. And then I opened my eyes, and had to adjust to the white, bright light that was shining down on me. I tried to think back to what had happened—to what I remembered before everything went black. Ian had been drugging me. He had been causing the hallucinations. He had been putting something in my tea, which I had so carelessly allowed him to make for me. Ian had said that Bridget was coming home and then I had seen Bessie. And then I made the connection. Oh God. Had I done something to Bridget? Had I confused her for Bessie because of the hallucinations? Because of whatever Ian had plunged into my neck with his syringe.

As everything came back into focus, I tried to make sense of where I was. I realized I was no longer in our apartment. It looked like I was in some sort of hospital.

"Hello, Abigail."

I turned my head to the sound of the voice—it was Dr. Aldridge. He was standing in the entryway of the room I was in. He looked as if he had been called in late in the evening and had haphazardly thrown some clothes on.

"Doctor," I said curtly.

Dr. Aldridge stepped into the waiting room and took a seat next to me. He didn't look at me right away—he just sat there, staring off into the distance, thinking perhaps.

"Mr. Cross called me upon your arrival to the hospital tonight," he spoke. "He informed me of what happened, and as soon he told me, he wished he hadn't."

"And what exactly did Ian tell you, Doctor?"

"He said that you attacked him and Miss Ward in your home," Aldridge answered. "He said that you threw Bridget to the floor. She has a mild head injury, and a small cut, but she will be okay."

"And did Ian tell you how he has been drugging me for the past four months?" I asked. "Did he tell you the name of the drug he's been putting into my tea—the drug that has been inducing my hallucinations? Did he tell you about the drug he plunged into my

159

neck tonight, only moments after calling Bridget home, telling her I had been causing a scene in the kitchen? Did he elaborate on any of that, Doctor?"

Dr. Aldridge considered me. "Mr. Cross did mention you might say something along those lines. He told me you were accusing him of doing things before you began attacking him."

I looked away and laughed. I laughed and laughed and laughed. I had allowed Ian to trick me into this. He had probably been planning on me finding all of the information he had been hiding. It would only add to his story of me being a crazy person when it all came out.

"You do know what this means, Abigail?"

I looked back into Aldridge's eyes. I did know what it meant. He was going to try and take me—to that *place*. My eyes shifted to the exit, and I thought about escaping. I might be able to do it. Dr. Aldridge was an older man—I could probably outrun him if I needed to. But it was then that I saw another person—a woman. She was doing her best to look inconspicuous, but I could tell she was with him. Every few seconds or so, I caught her gaze veering into the waiting room, waiting to see if she needed to intervene. I wouldn't get out of here without fighting my way out, and I had no idea if I would win that fight. It might only make things worse.

"I'm assuming I don't have a choice in the matter," I finally said to Aldridge.

"I'm afraid not," he replied. "And I think it would be best if we were to leave now before your friend Bridget is all stitched up. I don't know how she'll take it."

"Will she come visit though?" I asked.

"No," Aldridge said. "The facility doesn't allow for visitors because of the—well because of the nature of the majority of its clients. But you won't be there forever, Abigail. We need to get you through this, and you'll be as good as new."

This was exactly what Ian wanted. I had no idea whether Aldridge was in on it too, but I knew his statement, that this was temporary, wasn't true. Even if Aldridge intended on my eventual release, Ian wouldn't allow it. He would find some way for me to remain there until whatever plan he was concocting was completed.

"Can I make a call before we go?"

Aldridge smiled at that and then quickly shook his head. "I'm afraid not. You aren't really in the position of making demands, Abigail."

Might as well go out with a bang. I began to scream.

"Please, help me!" I shouted at the top of my longs. "Bridget! Bridget!"

It was only moments before Bridget appeared in the doorway, but Aldridge's assistant put a hand on her shoulder.

"What are you doing to her?" she asked.

"We need to take her, Miss Ward," Aldridge responded. "I'm sorry."

Aldridge's assistant moved past Bridget and into the room. She approached me and began to pull my arms behind my back to restrain me. I began to flail, attempting to get out of her grip. I knew it was no good, though. I only had moments left before they would put me out. Aldridge was already moving to a counter opposite me, pulling out a syringe and a bottle from a cabinet. I quickly looked to

Bridget.

"You have to believe me," I said to her.

Aldridge inserted the syringe into the bottle.

"Do not trust Ian. He's been lying to us."

The syringe began to pull the medicine into it.

"Get somewhere safe tonight."

A hand went over my mouth and I bit down on it. Aldridge's assistant screamed. Aldridge put the bottle down and began to move toward me.

"Go to the San Francisco Public Library and demand to see Thomas Jane," I screamed at Bridget. "Tell him wh—"

The needle plunged into my neck and everything went dark again.

Whatever Aldridge had given me, it didn't keep me out for long. I woke up in a car that was pulling into a hospital building. I looked at the sign by the road that read: *St. Ignatius's Hospital for the Unstable and Helpless.*

I stared aghast at the name of the hospital. The "unstable and helpless." I supposed that was me now. I needed help because I couldn't help myself, at least in the eyes of these people. The building was tall and had a rather gothic feel to it. I looked up and saw several floors rising from the ground. A very tall, wire fence surrounded the exterior of the hospital. Since I had been out on the way there, I had no idea how far from the city it was, but it looked as if it lay just outside of San Francisco, perched on a hill—looking out over the city in the distance.

"Welcome to your new home," Dr. Aldridge said from the

driver's seat, "temporarily, of course."

He drove the vehicle forward, slowly making the ascent up the hill toward the ostentatious building. As we got closer to the building, I began to feel unstable. I felt like darkness, worse than ever before, was penetrating me.

Dr. Aldridge and his assistant helped me out of the vehicle, and we made our way into the hospital. As soon as I walked through the door, I felt it. Evil. Hatred. Darkness. The voices of people in agony filled my head—people screaming in pain because of the terrible acts of another. Images flashed through my mind of all the terrible things people did in the world. I saw Hitler. I saw signs that read "concentration camps." I saw people being tortured—being gassed. I saw their bodies being incinerated all because they weren't like him. Piercing screams filled every part of my mind. I couldn't take it. I immediately turned and made a beeline for the door—the door that was now closing—shutting me off from the world.

I felt the thick arms of Aldridge's assistant trying to hold me in place as I screamed and screamed and screamed. I clawed at her hands. I needed to get away. In my peripheral vision, I saw Aldridge's hand go into his pocket and pull out a syringe and needle. Here we go again. I felt a stick in my side and then—nothing.

Just as I had succumbed to the darkness, I also awoke to it.

When my eyes finally opened, after what I only could imagine was several hours, I was in a pitch-black room, lying in a bed. My fingers brushed against the spot on my arm where Aldridge's assistant had administered a drug that had ended my attempted escape and put me into a sedated sleep. I had no idea what had happened. The only thing I knew was that as soon as I stepped into this building, I felt extreme, pure hatred. I still felt it. Strangely enough, it seemed like a buzz now. It was there, like a fly that keeps circling your head, refusing to leave you alone. But it wasn't overbearing now. It was tolerable. The idea of pure hatred being tolerable was even more unfathomable.

Suddenly, I heard locks clicking, and light poured into the room. I shielded my eyes from the light, having grown used to the darkness. After a few moments, I finally mustered the courage to open them. Dr. Aldridge stood in the doorway, a look of utmost concern on his face.

"Abigail," he said, "I'm sorry about having to sedate you earlier. I hope you understand, given the situation."

I didn't speak, only nodded.

"Very well," Aldridge continued. "I would like to show you to your new room."

I looked around in confusion, assuming this to be my new room, but Aldridge quickly shut that idea down.

"Oh, this isn't it," he said. "We simply put patients here when we believe them to be at risk to themselves or others. Before I take you to your new room though, our leading psychologist would like to have her first meeting with you."

"You won't be my doctor?" I asked him.

"I will be," Dr. Aldridge continued, "but Dr. Waters is responsible for the wellbeing of this hospital and its facilities. As part of her responsibilities, she meets with all new patients to discuss their plan of treatment and the options available for them. If you would follow me."

Dr. Aldridge led me out of the room, which I now realized was padded. For my protection, I guessed. Aldridge led me down an ominous hallway. The ceilings were high with light fixtures hanging from them. The hallway had the smell of a sterile hospital. Doors were on each side, each one locked and secured as I passed it. I passed nurses in white uniforms going from room to room to attend to the various needs of other patients. At the end of the hallway was a small flight of stairs that led up into a room with a grand staircase that led up to the entrances of the various floors of the hospital. We climbed and climbed and climbed until we reached the very last floor. Upon Dr. Aldridge unlocking and opening the door, I was immediately frustrated as before me lay yet another flight of stairs that led up to a single doorway.

"She's up there," he suddenly told me. "I will be down here waiting for you. Simply knock when you reach the top."

I nodded and began the climb. Behind me, I heard the door click shut and lock. I looked back at it and then forward again, unsure if I wanted to carry on. But there was no other way, so I did. When I finally reached the top, I extended my arm and knocked.

"Come in." It was a woman's voice; I assumed it could only be Dr. Waters.

I reached forward and opened the door. The room it led into was breathtaking. Before me was a room filled to the brim with books and strange looking instruments, as well as models of the human brain. Shelves upon shelves lined the walls. They stacked all the way to the ceiling. Various statues were around the room as well as pictures of the brain, together, taken apart, and studied. Straight ahead was a large oval window and through the window, I could see parts of the city. I still wasn't quite sure which part of the city we were in as I hadn't paid much attention to the drive, given the circumstances.

Before the window was a large oak desk and sitting at the desk was a woman with blonde, almost white, hair. Her hair fell just to the start of her neck, and she wore a pair of black spectacles. She was dressed in a professional manner—a black dress, and a white doctor's coat. There was something familiar about her; something about her features that tugged at my memory. But I couldn't quite figure it out. She smiled and stood up, walking toward me, her hand extended.

"You must be Abigail Jordan," she said. "It's truly a pleasure to meet you. My name is Dr. Karen Waters. Please, have a seat."

She beckoned toward the leather chair in front of her desk, and I took it. As Dr. Waters took her seat again, I admired her features. She was beautiful. It looked like the stressful career she had taken on had not affected her aging in the slightest. She looked to be in her mid-thirties. And there was something else. She carried a sort of resemblance to someone, but I couldn't put my finger on as to what.

"I trust you understand why it was best for you to come here," Dr. Waters began. She had her hands folded on her desk, enunciated every word clearly, and looked me directly in the eye when she spoke.

I really didn't understand why I was here except for Ian to achieve whatever he was planning. And as I thought about it now, I realized this woman could be behind it too. Treading carefully was important.

I nodded.

"You've undergone a great deal of emotional distress over the past year, I understand," she continued, now looking down at what I assumed to be my file. "It says here you relocated from London after losing your parents and your fiancé in the air raids." She looked back up at me, waiting for my response. I simply nodded again, and she continued. "Loss such as this can have devastating, even debilitating, effects on the human brain."

She closed the file and took off her glasses, again looking me directly in the eye.

"I want to help you, Abigail," Dr. Waters said, "but as I ask from all of my patients, I'm going to need you to put your trust in both my staff, as well as myself."

Trust. It brought back memories quickly—Bessie seeking my trust, me, unwilling to give it, until finally I did, and it backfired in my face. And again, with Ian, only to have it thrown back at me.

"I can't trust you," I responded.

To my surprise, Dr. Waters didn't appear to be taken aback by this. But after thinking about it for a moment, why would she? I'm sure most of her patients would find it difficult to come into this place, a place labeled for the unstable, and then be asked to trust the leading authority. She simply smiled.

"I wouldn't expect you to," she said. "After all, we've only just met. But over time, maybe. I'm excited to begin your treatment tomorrow, Abigail. For now, I think we will continue your treatment using amobarbital. However, we will definitely increase the dosage."

"I don't know if that is something I would be interested in," I said. I had no idea if this was what Ian had been using to drug me, but if it was, I knew that it would only make things worse. I continued, "I wasn't a fan of being put on medication in the first place. Is an increase in dosage really necessary? I thought that was something used for more extreme cases."

"Would you not call yourself an extreme case?" Dr. Waters asked me.

"I mean it's not like I'm always lashing out and being aggressive," I responded. "I know that I've had a few incidences where I have, but I don't know if an increase in medication is something that needs to happen."

I thought about mentioning the fact that Ian had been drugging me, but decided against it. It would only put another nail in my coffin.

"I completely understand where you are coming from, Abigail," Dr. Waters continued, "but, unfortunately, it really isn't up to you. I'm afraid you will have to let us decide what is best for you. We won't make any decisions lightly.

"Now, we need to discuss your living arrangements. I like to run things in a different manner, compared to my other colleagues in this profession. You have full access to every room in this building, at all times. We will never keep you locked in your room, unless you give us a reason to. Every exit in the building will be monitored, twenty-four hours a day. If, for some reason, a person is able to get out, they will still have to get through our strict security measures that surround the grounds of the building, and, of course, they will have to get over the wall that surrounds the entire campus. We do have a few rules we expect you to follow: the first rule is that you are to report to all meals on time. Breakfast is at eight o'clock in the morning, with lunch at noon, and dinner at seven o'clock. All times are strictly enforced. Furthermore, there is a mandatory therapy session every day from one o'clock in the afternoon to two o'clock in the afternoon. Do you have any questions?"

I didn't respond; I simply stared at her. How had I allowed myself to get into this position? I hoped to God Bridget had at least tried to contact Thomas. Or maybe Elijah was aware of my situation and was putting together a rescue plan at this very moment. Even though I knew the hallucinations had been induced by drugs, I had still had my own personal issues, and I knew this place would do more harm than good.

CHAPTER FIFTEEN

The hallways at St. Ignatius's were cold and dreary. I wore a sweater around the building because I constantly felt chilly. While the hospital was run by Dr. Waters, it was also a convent that housed several Catholic nuns. A Catholic priest also came by, on a weekly basis, for Sunday mass and confession. Because I had not been to church or confession recently, and because I felt it would add something to my life I had been missing, I decided to take the opportunity.

As soon as I sat down in the confessional, memories of St. Patrick's in Soho came soaring back to me. For a moment, I felt overwhelmed and unable to continue, but I closed my eyes, took several deep breaths, and then I was fine.

The window of the confessional opened and I knew it was my time to speak.

"Forgive me, Father, for I have sinned," I began, the words flowing back to me as if I had been here only yesterday, "it has been several months since my last confession."

I began to list my sins and I was surprised to find there weren't many. My main sin was not attending church every Sunday, or on the holy days of obligation. The priest heard my confession and then gave me my penance, but I didn't let him go just yet.

"Father?"

"Yes, child?"

"I know you don't know me, but I was wondering if you could offer some advice?"

Before I knew it, I had spilled everything to him, with the exception of being a Timekeeper. I knew a priest couldn't reveal my confession to anyone, but I really didn't want him to go off thinking I was truly crazy. Then again, I was in a mental institution. I told him about Phillip's death, as well as my parents and Mrs. Baxter. I told him about moving to San Francisco and feeling depressed and unable to move on. Again though, I left out the hallucinations. That had not been me. That had been Ian and part of his plan.

"I realize this is a lot of information," I said. "I guess I just don't know where to go from here."

"I think what you are doing right now is the answer," he responded. "Coming back to God and Jesus Christ, and letting them take on your pain and sorrow is what you are supposed to do. Continue coming to church and saying your prayers and know God gives us personal trials in life and you will be rewarded for it in heaven."

He almost took my breath away. It was the same advice my mother had always given me. It was advice that had always been tucked away in the back of my head, but advice I had not looked back on in such a long time.

"Thank you, Father," I said. After that, I stood up to leave. I prayed my penitence in the chapel and after that, I sat there for a long time.

* * *

Later that day, I ended up back in the room I had been assigned. It wasn't much. There was a bed, a nightstand with a lamp, and a small desk and chair. There wasn't anywhere for clothes as a clean pair of the hospital clothes I was given to wear were brought to me each morning; the old ones collected to be washed.

I spent most of the day lying in my bed, staring up at the ceiling. I hadn't had much of an episode since they had brought me here, so I assumed the medication they had been giving me was not the same as what Ian had been drugging me with. What was the point of actually giving me hallucinations anymore anyway? I was already here. Plan accomplished.

Come to me.

I sat up in my bed and looked around the room. It was her. Melanie.

I'm here. In this building. I've always been here.

Melanie was here. Was she part of the plan? She had to have been. Ian had known about her. He implied that he even had a thing for her when he had attacked me. Was he keeping her here against her will? Was he keeping her hostage? Or was she here on her own accord?

Come to the lowest level.

I could either sit in my bed and be compliant, or I could find answers.

I chose to find answers.

The halls were almost completely dark except for the moonlight that seeped in through the windows. I was surprised to find it was night and everyone had gone to bed. I found it strange I was allowed to roam the building as I pleased, but remembered what Dr. Waters had said. There were always people watching, and even if I managed to somehow get out of the building, I still had to get over the wall surrounding the grounds.

Turn left.

This was entirely too creepy. I knew it was her, but it still made me cringe. It still sent shivers down my spine. I turned left and found myself descending a flight of stairs. As I went further and further down, the temperature got colder and colder. I hugged my arms to myself as I continued to make my descent, until, finally, I was before a single, plain, wooden door.

In the middle of the door was a small window that could be unlatched and opened. I reached up, undid the hook, and pulled open the little window. I could now see into the room beyond.

The room was a decent size but it wasn't well lit. I could see a bed on the other side of the room as well as a bookshelf along one wall. There were loads and loads of books that would easily entertain whoever lived in this room for quite a while.

"Hello?" I called into the room.

There was no response, but I could swear I heard someone breathing. I looked down at the handle and tried to pull open the door, but there was no such luck. The door was locked. It was either meant to keep someone out or someone in, maybe both. I scanned the room again through the little window, paying close attention to everything I saw. It was then that I saw it. Because of the darkness in the room, I could barely make it out. But it was there—the shadow of a person—in the farthest corner of the room.

"Who are you?" I asked. "Did you call me to this room? Is it you? Are you Melanie?"

"Yes."

The voice sounded hoarse, but it also sounded familiar. It sounded like I had heard it before. It sounded like my own voice.

"Will you please come out of the shadows?" I asked.

The person hesitated, but then finally, they did. And even though I knew it would be someone who looked exactly like me, even though I knew it was my twin, everything I knew about the world seemed to flip upside down. When the person finally stepped out of the shadows, it was like looking into a mirror. My sister didn't look starved. She didn't look like she was being held against her will. She looked entirely comfortable in here.

"What are you doing down here?"

I turned and saw the woman who had assisted Aldridge in bringing me here. She ran down the steps and turned to me.

"You shouldn't be down here."

She looked at the door, and at Melanie, who was looking out through the little window.

"Go back into your corner," the woman said. "Now. I can't shut the window until you are back into your corner."

Melanie smiled at the woman, then turned and gave me a wink. She disappeared into the shadows once more. Aldridge's assistant leaned on her tiptoes to try and see over the window. When she was satisfied Melanie was out of the way, she stepped forward and reached out to close the window. And then Melanie's arm shot out of the little window, grabbing the woman by her hair and pulling her up against the door. The woman screamed, trying to break free, but the window was big enough that Melanie was able to tear a bit of the woman's flesh away from her ear.

I screamed in horror and ran forward, trying to help the woman.

"Let go of her," I shouted. "Please, let go of her."

Melanie finally let go of the woman's hair and she fell backward on top of me. I pushed her over to the side and leaned over her to assess the damage. She was bleeding profusely from the ear. I put pressure to the wound and looked back at the stairs I'd come down.

"Someone help!" I shouted. "Please!"

Behind me, I heard cackling. Melanie was laughing at the top of her lungs. It was a hideous laugh. A cold laugh. And then I realized, that feeling I had had as soon as I entered the hospital. The feeling of cold, death, anger, hatred. That had come from her. This girl, my sister, was evil.

CHAPTER SIXTEEN

At some point, other nurses had come to assist me. But for whatever reason, they assumed I had caused the damage and I was rewarded with another stick in the neck. I awoke later, tied to a chair, in what I could only assume was Melanie's room. There was more light in the room now, and as I looked around, I could see there were more books then I had previously thought. Bookshelves lined the walls, filled to the brim with books. I wondered what it would be like, to be held here against your will, but to be fed, taken care of, and given books to entertain you.

Directly in front of me, Melanie was seated, cross-legged, on her bed. Her head was slightly cocked to the side as she observed me. She looked exactly like me, with the exception that her hair was much longer. It fell all the way down her back whereas mine only came to just below my shoulders.

"What was it like?" she asked me.

I looked at her in confusion. What was what like? Furthermore, why was I tied to a chair in her bedroom? Why had they put me unconscious with another drug?

"What are you talking about?" I asked her.

She took a deep breath before speaking. "I mean, what's it like to grow up out there?" She gestured toward the wall, as if there were a window there that led to the outside world, but there wasn't.

"Have you grown up here?" I asked not answering her question. I needed to know. "How long have you been here?"

But before she answered, I remembered what Ian had said that day in the library. He had not only called me Melanie, he had asked what I was doing out. He had told me then. She had always been locked up somewhere.

"No," Melanie replied. "I've been moved from place to place. But it's always been pretty similar to this. Now, what's it like, out there?"

"I don't really know how to describe it," I answered. "I really haven't lived a different way, so I can't compare it to anything else."

She moved off her bed and stood, walking toward me. She was barefoot and the only thing she wore was a long, white hospital gown that fell to the floor. I realized, to my horror, that she carried a knife with her. What kind of hospital was this?

"I just find it a little unfair," she said, stopping in front of me and falling to her knees, "that you got to live out there these eighteen, almost nineteen, years, whereas I had to stay cooped up inside. Not always here, of course, but in other places."

"I'm sorry that happened to you," I said. "I honestly don't know why it happened. I didn't even know you existed until very recently."

"You need to be punished," Melanie answered.

And then she stabbed her knife into my leg. I let out a howling scream of pain, biting my lip so hard as I did that I cut it open as well.

"What are you doing?" I shouted at her.

Melanie gripped the knife hard and pulled it out just as the door to the room opened. I looked up to see Ian walking in, along with Dr. Aldridge and Dr. Waters. Just as I had suspected, Dr. Aldridge was involved. And Waters too, apparently.

"That's enough, Melanie," Dr. Waters said, closing the door behind her and locking it with a key.

Melanie took one look at Dr. Waters and ran back to her bed. She was scared of her. I could tell just by looking into her eyes.

Dr. Waters walked toward me, her heels clicking against the floor.

"What are we going to do with you, Miss Jordan?" Dr. Waters asked. "I thought having you in this hospital would keep you contained enough, but you are still persistent in putting your nose in places it does not belong."

"Technically," I responded, "you did say I could go anywhere in the hospital."

Dr. Waters smiled at that.

"You're just as cheeky as your mother," she responded.

"You knew my mother?"

Dr. Waters began laughing at that. She cackled and looked to Ian and Dr. Aldridge.

"What do you say, gentlemen?" she asked them. "Shall we lay all the cards on the table?"

Dr. Waters turned to me, studying me.

"Of course, I knew your mother," she said. "I did give birth to her after all."

And then the conversation I had with Elijah only the day before yesterday came back to me.

"Our mother, she is the exact opposite of what a mother should be," he had said. "And I know she is behind this. She knows that you exist, and she will stop at nothing."

This woman, Dr. Waters, was my grandmother. But she couldn't be. She didn't look any older than maybe forty. And my own mother, she would be around that age.

"That's not possible," I said.

Dr. Waters smiled again. "Oh, it is very much possible. You see with the forbidden powers, I can live forever."

The forbidden powers. I had not given much thought to them over the last several months. I hadn't felt the need to. My training had told me no one possessed them, but then I learned that wasn't true when Bessie gained the powers the night she died. Now it seemed like everything I had been taught was a lie.

"But my father, Mathias, he said very few people have gained the powers. And now you, and Bessie before you."

Dr. Waters cackled again. "Please, Abigail. You are part of a plan that has been in place since the beginning of our history, of our people. I, along with my associates, have taken great care in making sure our plans have been conducted in secret. We've carefully spent time infiltrating the Council to ensure our plans will come to fruition. It's easy for our society to say no one has ever achieved such a thing as those powers, but in all honesty, who would come forward to say that they have achieved them? They are *forbidden* after all.

"Regardless, you are the key to fulfilling the prophecy. The prophecy states that two Timekeeping twins will be born into the original family to rule over the Timekeeping world. They will bring darkness into our world and move the Timekeepers into a new age. But, unfortunately, you haven't been very compliant, even with the drugs we have been using on you. So, what could we possibly do to make sure that you won't be a problem in the future?"

She looked over to Dr. Aldridge and he stepped forward, speaking up.

"We have a number of sedatives on hand here at the hospital," he suggested. "We probably should have used them from the beginning. We can take her upstairs and keep her heavily sedated until the time comes."

The time comes. I had no idea what that meant, but I didn't want to find out.

Dr. Waters nodded. "That will work. Dr. Aldridge, please prep Miss Jordan."

With that, Dr. Waters, my grandmother, turned on her heel and left the room, leaving me with Ian, Aldridge, and my sister. Aldridge took a syringe from his pocket and stuck it in the side of my neck. And once again, I returned to the darkness.

When I awoke I was tied to a bed. The only thing I could see was the ceiling above me and I was conscious of the fact that the bed was moving. I guessed I was on a gurney, being led to the room where they would heavily sedate me. I still couldn't speak. I was barely aware of what was going on.

Finally, the gurney was pushed through a set of double doors into what looked like a room where a surgery would be performed.

"Abigail," a man said. "Can you hear me?"

I turned my head slightly and saw an older man looking down at me.

"My name is Dr. Jonas," the man said. "I will be administering your medications."

"Frauds," I managed to say. "Dr. Waters and Aldridge are frauds. I don't need this."

"Abigail," Dr. Jonas said, "listen to me very carefully. We are going to make you better. These drugs will help you not be suspicious of everyone around you anymore. Won't that be great? It will just be you again." The doctor looked up at someone else and then said, "if you will."

I shook my head, but he wasn't listening and I was still tied to the table. And then the strangest thing happened. Elijah was suddenly leaning over me. Was this part of the drug they had given me? Or was he truly here now? I knew he was there when he reached up to his mouth with just one finger, signaling for me to not say a word. And that's what I did.

Elijah put a mask over my face, but I didn't feel anything come out of it. Dr. Jonas turned back to me to see if I was under and then Elijah was behind him and then Dr. Jonas was gone. A few moments passed until the mask was lifted off of my face and Elijah was undoing the restraints that held me down to the table. As soon as the restraints were off, I sat up.

"You found me," I said to him.

Elijah nodded. "Your friend, Bridget Ward, grew suspicious and contacted Thomas at his work location. I had already had a premonition about you and I contacted him immediately to tell him I would take care of it. It was surprisingly easy to impersonate a doctor's assistant in this place. But anyway, that's a story for later. We need to get you out of here. Now. Unfortunately, I'm going to need you to lay back down and pretend to be dead. That will be the fastest way to get you out of here."

I nodded and lay back on the table. Elijah covered his face with a surgical mask and found a sheet, but before placing it over me, he looked down at me. "Abigail, I need you to trust me, no matter what happens. Okay?"

"Okay," I said.

He laid the sheet over my face and then the gurney began to move again. I felt the gurney being pushed through the double doors of the procedure room again and we were traveling down a hall. I waited underneath the sheet, completely still, trying not to make a sound.

"Excuse me," a woman said, "what happened?"

"Dead," I heard Elijah say.

"Unfortunate."

Elijah agreed and then the gurney kept moving. We turned several corners before stopping.

"You're doing great," Elijah said. "We are in the lift, going down."

As soon as the doors opened again and Elijah pushed the gurney out, there was shouting.

"There was an attack in the procedure room," I heard someone saying.

"A doctor's been attacked," someone else said.

"There's an imposter in the hospital," a third voice said.

I tried to stifle a laugh at that last statement. There was more than one imposter in this hospital. The gurney began to travel faster and I could tell Elijah was getting nervous. We turned several more corners and then finally went through another set of doors and I felt cold air against my skin. We were outside. Elijah pulled the sheet off of me and I sat up.

"Follow me," he said. "Now."

I looked to my right to see a row of cars. I assumed this was some sort of parking lot for hospital employees. I followed Elijah to an old Cadillac and stood by the passenger side door while he leaned across the seat and unlocked the door.

"Stop them!"

I looked up and saw Dr. Waters running out of the back entrance, her heels clicking against the pavement as she ran. Everything was happening so fast. She started to raise her hand, perhaps to use her powers, but in broad daylight?

The door pushed open.

"Get in!"

I got in the car and before I even had the door pulled shut, it was skidding backward. Elijah clearly didn't care if he ran over his mother. And then we were speeding forward, out of the employee parking lot, and on to the streets of San Francisco flying at the highest speed possible toward what I assumed would be the closest entrance to the San Francisco Headquarters.

CHAPTER SEVENTEEN

Elijah successfully got me back to the Headquarters. While it was inevitably better than staying at St. Ignatius's, I was still constantly reminded I was in hiding. I had to stay away from Ian. Thomas was doing his best to keep Ian out, but he couldn't exactly go to the Council with the issue considering Dr. Waters had people of her own on there. While staying at the Headquarters was the safest option for me right now, it didn't really matter. If Ian wanted to come here and get me, he would. Luckily, I didn't have to worry about Bridget. After she had grown concerned and contacted Thomas, he made plans for her to move into the American Headquarters where she would be safe from Ian as well. I hadn't seen her since I'd been back, but I could only imagine how she was handling this realization about him.

My biological mother had done even more for me than I had previously thought. She had been trying to protect me from this prophecy, from me meeting my sister, as well as my grandmother. And she had succeeded, until I ran into Ian at that library. It had all been coincidental, entirely coincidental. If I had not been there that day, I wondered if life would have turned out differently. I wondered if my parents would still be here, if Phillip would still be here.

I sat on the couch in Thomas' study. Elijah had just brought me into the room, and Thomas was sitting next to me, his arm around me.

"We should go talk," Elijah said to Thomas.

I looked up at Elijah. "Whatever you need to say, you can say it here in front of me. Now is the time to start explaining."

Elijah sighed. "You're right." He pulled the armchair near the couch directly in front of me and sat down.

"By now, you probably know the woman you met at that hospital is my mother."

I nodded. "Dr. Karen Waters."

Elijah shook his head. "That isn't her real name. The real Dr. Karen Waters died a few years ago and spent her life working at a mental institution in New York. My mother has been impersonating her, and using her credentials to gain access here in San Francisco. Her real name is Lucinda Callaghan.

"I've been tracking my mother for some time, attempting to find out her true intentions. I'm still in the dark about this prophecy, but I can tell you, based on what I observed at the hospital, keeping you alive is one of the key components of it. If you died, well, it sounds like there wouldn't be a prophecy anymore. I can also assume it has to do with having twins, identical twins to be exact. As I told you before, my mother has always hated me, and now I know why. She was hoping to fulfill this prophecy with her children, and when she birthed two girls, I'm sure she was over the moon about it. My nana, really the woman who raised me and protected me from my mother, said my mother was furious when a third baby was delivered that day. It all makes sense now. And I believe she has infiltrated the

Timekeeping Council and has been doing so for quite some time."

"Headrick," I said. "She has to be behind this. She was the sole reason I was brought to San Francisco, where this Lucinda, my grandmother, would be conveniently located. My transfer shouldn't have even involved Headrick, yet it did."

"Be that as it may," Thomas said, "we still don't have any proof. We can't make allegations against Headrick, the woman holding the highest position in our world, without first having proof."

"If the Council is infiltrated though," I said, "then that would explain the death of Winston. We still don't know who did it and it couldn't have been Bessie. Even in the end, she still didn't know how to get into the London Headquarters. It makes sense it could have been Ian, but what if it wasn't?"

"That might be a possibility," Elijah continued, "but give me some time. Let me see what I can find out. But for now, be safe."

Elijah smiled at me and then stood up and exited the room. Thomas and I sat in silence for a few moments until he finally spoke.

"Abby, I was so scared when they took you. Ian wouldn't give me any information about what happened. If Elijah hadn't found you, I don't know what would have happened. Can I be honest with you about something?"

I didn't respond. I only nodded.

"The way that I feel about you right now," he said, "I've never felt that way about anyone."

I looked at him. This man, this man who only months ago I had assumed treated women like objects to be had, rather than human beings to be loved, cared for, and respected, was telling me he had changed. And he was telling me that he had changed for me. He could have been lying, but I believed him. And I knew that I reciprocated the feelings, but I had been trying to push them away out of respect for Phillip. Even though Phillip wanted me to go on with life.

"I can never stop loving him," I said. "Phillip, I mean. He will always be there, no matter how much time goes by."

"I would never ask you to stop loving him," Thomas said. "*Never.*"

Something in me was shifting. This darkness I had experienced for so long was breaking down. It was still there, but it wasn't as powerful. And I knew it was because of the man sitting in front of me. Hot, salty tears were pouring down my cheeks now and my vision was becoming blurry as I looked at him.

"Did I upset you?" Thomas asked.

I shook my head, and said the only two words that made sense. The only thing I wanted right now.

"Kiss me."

He looked at me for a moment, and then he moved forward on the couch and took my face in his hands and he kissed me. It was just a kiss. He did it and then he pulled away and looked at me, as if he was asking my permission. I nodded and he leaned in and pressed his lips to mine, his tongue brushing mine. It was passionate, tender, loving. He slowly lowered me onto the couch and was on top of me, moving his rough hands through my hair, carefully holding the back of my head as he continued to kiss me. It was a moment I wanted to last forever.

* * *

I woke up the next morning on the couch in Thomas' study. A blanket had been draped over me and Thomas was gone. I took a minute to force my thoughts to go back to the previous evening. We had only kissed, and then he had stayed with me for a while until I finally fell asleep.

"Abigail."

I sat up. Phillip was standing across the room. Dried blood was on his face from a gash in his head. He looked distraught.

"Phillip." It barely came off my lips, but I said it.

"What have you done?"

"I didn't do anything," I said. "You're not real. You're dead."

"You've betrayed me," Phillip replied. "Why did you betray me?"

I stood up and marched over to him, or whatever this thing that was talking to me was.

"No," I said. "I didn't betray you. You're dead, Phillip. I don't even know if it's really you I'm talking to right now, but you told me you wanted me to move on. You wanted me to live my life."

"How could you?"

I fell to my knees. Tears were pouring from my eyes now. I moved my hands up over my ears so that I wouldn't have to listen to Phillip, or whatever this thing was, speak to me.

"Go away!" I shouted. I closed my eyes, continuing to cover my ears. But it didn't do anything.

"You are a killer. Killer. Killer. Killer."

It repeated the words over and over and over again. No matter what I did, no matter how much I tried to ignore it, I couldn't.

"Go away!"

I stood up and grabbed the nearest thing I could find—a vase on a side table. I threw it at Phillip and it went right through him, slamming against the stone wall and shattering into pieces. Shards of glass went flying, right through Phillip. Nothing seemed to get rid of him.

But then the room dissolved and I was on the Golden Gate Bridge. And she was there. In that white dress, her arm extended out to me, hand open. She was there, just like she always had been. And I had the sense that danger was coming. And then the waves from the bay washed her away.

"Abby!"

My eyes burst open and Thomas was above me. I sat up and fell into his arms. It had been a dream, just a dream. I cried in Thomas' arms. I was still punishing myself for falling in love again. I also cried because I was glad it had just been a dream this time. Ian was no longer there to drug me, and make me see things that weren't there. He could no longer make me question reality versus fantasy. And because of that, I was okay, at least for now.

CHAPTER EIGHTEEN

I found Bridget in the spare bedroom Thomas had lent to her since we could no longer return to our apartment at the Chambord Building. She was sitting in a chair in front of the room's vanity desk attempting to brush her hair, but as she pulled the brush down and through her hair, her arm shook a little. Her eyes were red, indicating she had been crying.

I pushed the room's door in further and shut it behind me. She looked up when the door closed, saw me, and then turned back to the mirror, continuing her attempts at brushing her hair. I sat on the edge of her bed, looking at her.

"Bridget," I said. "I just want you to know I understand what you are going through. This is the second time someone has betrayed me like this. I know it hurts, and it's confusing, and you don't even understand how it can be possible. But the unfortunate thing about it is that people do this all the time. They betray us. They take advantage of our kindness and the things that make us who we are.

"Don't let yourself be consumed by this. I'm begging you. Ian isn't worth it. He's a terrible person, and I understand your pain. You will find someone else. I *promise* that you will."

Bridget slowly put the brush down on the vanity table, closed her eyes for a moment, and took a deep breath. Then, she turned in her chair to look at me.

"It hurts," she said, "that Ian betrayed me. It really, really does. But that isn't what is bothering me right now."

"What is it?" I asked.

"Do you remember that day at the Tadich Grill?" Bridget asked. "I told you that there was something that I needed to tell you, but that I wasn't ready."

I did remember. Even thought it had only been a few months ago, it felt like it had been forever, given everything that had happened.

"I do," I said, nodding. "Do you want to tell me now?"

"Yes," Bridget said. "I do."

She stood up and paced around the room. I could tell she was trying to come up with the right thing to say; the right way to approach the issue. Finally, she took a deep breath and looked back up at me.

"I've always been blunt with you," Bridget said. "I've never sugarcoated anything, so there is no reason I should sugarcoat my own business. Abigail, I'm sexually attracted to women."

"Oh," I said. I was surprised. I could tell Bridget was afraid I would react in a negative way, or treat her as if she were inferior to me. But that wasn't the way my parents raised me. They raised me to respect people, and to tolerate their decisions, even if I personally disagreed with those decisions. I was not the one to judge. But honestly, at the end of the day, even if it went against what I believed in, I didn't personally disagree with this. Because it wasn't Bridget's *decision*. It wasn't her *choice*. It was the way she was, regardless of what anyone wanted to say otherwise. You can't change what you feel, just like you can't change the color of your skin, or the ancestors that you are descended from. Just like I couldn't change being a Timekeeper. I had tried to run away from it. I couldn't do that. I had to accept it, live with it, and make my choices around it. I truly believed God made us all a certain way. And if anyone disagreed with that, and who Bridget truly was, they could take their self-righteousness and go elsewhere.

"I'm happy for you then," I replied.

"You aren't upset?" Bridget asked. "You don't want to stop being my friend?"

"No, Bridget. You will always be my closest friend, and I will always accept you for being you. You've accepted me, and who I am, so why shouldn't I do the same?"

Bridget plopped down on the bed next to me and laid on her back, staring up the ceiling. I fell back and stared up at it as well.

"I didn't exactly accept you right away though," Bridget said.

I rolled onto my side and looked at her. She did the same and we were looking into each other's eyes. It reminded me of our childhood together. We used to sit out in my mother's garden and just stare at each other, giggle, and talk about things.

"Bridget," I said, "it is a little bit different. I mean you had to genuinely come to an understanding that I wasn't going insane. But the thing is, you did come to an understanding."

"Only after I saw and heard things though."

"Stop, Bridget," I said. "You are accepting. You accepted me.

And I accept you."

Tears were welling up in her eyes. She sat up and attempted to wipe them away. I sat up beside her and pulled her to me. She threw her arms around me and cried into my shoulder for a moment. I didn't know if her tears were of happiness about our friendship, sadness about everything that had happened to us, or something else. Maybe they were a combination of everything. In that moment, we had each other, and that was all we needed.

But the moment ended almost as quickly as it began.

"I really need to get to class," Bridget said, pulling away from me. She began to get up and move about the room, collecting together some of her things that she might need.

"Bridget," I said, "you can't go. It's not safe."

"Abby," Bridget responded, "I understand that. But I can't live my life underground, and you can't always be there to protect me. And I know Thomas doesn't think it's safe for you out there either, but sometimes, you just have to take a chance. How else are you going to live and experience life?"

She was right. It wasn't good for me to stay hidden away here, only because I was afraid of Ian, or Aldridge.

"I'll see you later," Bridget said. I looked up, nodded and smiled, and she left the room, leaving me there thinking about how I could get through all of this.

As much as I understood Bridget's reasons not to stay cooped up in the Headquarters all day, I began to worry when she did not return at the usual time from her classes. I paced back and forth in the room I had been staying in, waiting for her to get back. I constantly checked the pocket watch I had been given at my initiation for the time. It was getting later and later. Sighing, I finally made up my mind that something wasn't right and went to seek out Thomas.

Alma was in Thomas' study looking over some papers at his desk and writing down notes on a separate sheet of paper. She looked up as I walked into the room and smiled at me. I smiled back, but a quick flash distracted my attention. It was light flashing off of Thomas' blade above the fireplace. The blade that had been in his family for years. I tore my attention from it and looked back to Alma.

"Abby," she said, as friendly as ever, "how have you been doing, given everything?"

"It's been…" I hesitated, not able to find the words to describe being utterly betrayed for the second time in my life. After a moment, I quickly added, "Hectic."

Alma nodded in understanding. "Well, is there something I can do for you?"

"I'm looking for Thomas," I replied. "I'm getting a little worried about Bridget. She went out to attend her classes and hasn't returned yet. This is later than usual for her."

A look of concern flashed over face. "Well, Thomas had to leave on some business. He should be back soon though. If you want, I can send him a quick message?" She pulled out her pocket watch, ready to send a message, but I quickly shook my head.

"It's okay," I said. "I'm sure I'm just overthinking things."

Alma smiled and then the clicking of heels against the floor pulled our attention to the entrance study. Councilor Headrick walked through the entrance. She looked the same as always. Her hair was pulled back into a tight bun and she wore a dress similar to the one she'd worn at Mathias' hearing, one that looked as if it were swallowing her whole.

"Alma," Headrick said. "Have you made any headway on that report yet?"

"I'm working on it now," Alma replied.

"Good." Headrick turned her attention to me and smiled. "Miss Jordan." It was all she said, but it was layered with poison. I wanted to know what she was doing here. Where was the councilor who was actually in charge of the American Headquarters?

She looked away from me, and then her attention fell on Thomas' sword.

"I've always been fascinated by that sword," Headrick said. "Well, I'll be around the Headquarters today if you two should need anything. Goodbye."

Headrick turned on her heel and walked away. I looked back at Alma who had continued working on her report.

"Are you sure you don't want me to send Thomas a message?" she asked.

"No, no," I said. "It's fine. I might go and just run by her university for a bit."

Alma looked up at that. "Are you sure that's a good idea? I don't mean to be telling you what to do, but just considering everything."

"I'll be fine," I replied. "Just tell Thomas I went to look for her if he comes back."

Alma smiled at me and nodded. I left the room before I could change my mind and tell her to contact Thomas, or before she could tell me this might be a bad idea. I hoped it wasn't. I hoped I was overreacting. I hoped that Bridget was okay. And I hoped that Headrick was only here on business, but a nagging feeling told me that she wasn't.

The campus of the University of San Francisco was filled with students moving about their days, going home after their afternoon classes or finding the building for their evening classes. I pulled my coat tighter around myself as the fall air was a bit chillier today. I was on the main campus, and I had no idea where to go. I had already gone to the building Bridget went to her for her last class, which would have ended two hours or so ago. I racked my brain thinking about where she could possibly go on campus. Then, it came to me. The library. I wanted to punch myself for not thinking of it earlier. She had to be there. I was still familiar with the campus from my brief attendance and quickly made my way to the library, searching each row of shelves. Finally, I found her in the back, sitting alone, reading *A Tale of Two Cities*. Why did that book keep popping into my life?

I slowly approached the table, pulled out a chair and sat down. Bridget looked up at me and smiled.

"Well, hello there," she said, closing her book. And then she saw the look of concern on my face and added, "What's wrong?"

"You didn't come back from your class right away and I was worried."

Bridget sighed. "Abby, I'm only reading. I understand your

concern, but I'm fine. Honestly."

"Well, I'd feel a lot better if I could stay with you the rest of the day."

Bridget smiled, reaching out her hand and clasping mine. "That would be just fine. How about we go down to the pier and admire the scenic views?"

I giggled and then quickly put my hand over my mouth, looking around to see if I had disturbed anyone, but no one was paying any attention.

"I'd like that," I finally said. She smiled, packed up her things, and we headed to the pier.

"It's quite beautiful here, don't you think?" Bridget asked.

We were standing at the edge of the pier, looking out at the Bay. In the distance, we could see Alcatraz Prison standing on its island, filled with prisoners. Boats could be seen arriving at their port. We could also see the Golden Gate Bridge in the distance.

"It is," I responded. "But I do miss home sometimes." Not sometimes, but really a lot of the time.

"I know," Bridget said, leaning into me and putting her arm around my shoulder.

I hadn't thought about home in a long time. Most of my focus had been on the people I had lost, but I had also lost my home. The home I had grown up in for eighteen years had been destroyed by the air raids. The London Library, that held countless memories of spending time with Phillip, had suffered the same fate. And then there was the London Headquarters, my last possible place of refuge.

But I had been taken from there as well. San Francisco wasn't a terrible place to live by any means, but it wasn't my home. It wasn't where I was from. And the fact that many of the places I had called home in London weren't even there anymore, or were damaged beyond repair, made it all the worse.

"Yes, I'm kind of homesick too," said Ian.

It took a second for the voice to register. *Ian.* I turned and before I could do or say anything, he had pulled Bridget away from me. His hand was placed behind her back as if they were a couple simply taking a late afternoon stroll.

"Say or do anything," Ian said, "and the knife in my hand goes into her flesh. Understand?"

I nodded.

Bridget attempted to move away, and then suddenly let out a cry of pain Ian quickly cut off by covering her mouth with his other hand.

"The rules apply to you too, Bridget," Ian said. "Now you've made me stick you with the knife. I can push it in further, or you can cooperate and I'll take it out. Are you going to cooperate?"

Bridget nodded, tears forming in her eyes. Ian lowered his hand from her mouth, looked around to make sure he hadn't drawn any attention, and then looked back to me.

"Bridget and I are going for a little walk," Ian finally said. "I think you're familiar with our destination."

"Just take me," I said. "*Please.* Everything you are working toward has to do with me. Why do you need her?"

"I'm not arguing with you, Abigail," Ian said. "You know where to find her. Give it an hour before you come. Try and follow me, and she dies. Bring anyone but yourself, and she dies. Call out for help as we walk away, and she dies. I'm not above stabbing a woman to death in the street, Abigail. I've done a lot worse in my lifetime. Do you understand?"

"You're a psychopath," I said through clenched teeth.

"Thank you for that assessment," Ian said. "It's probably true, but it isn't what I asked you. Do *you* understand?"

I took a deep breath and then said, "Yes."

"Good," Ian said. "We will be seeing you then. One hour."

"Abby," Bridget said, "Don't trust him. Just go get h—"

Bridget let out another cry of pain from the knife going deeper into her skin.

"The same goes for you, darling," Ian whispered against her earlobe before nibbling on it a bit.

"Don't touch her!" I spat.

"Shut it," Ian said. "Both of you. Let's go."

He pulled Bridget with him and they walked away. I stood there, watching them go, while trying to come up with a plan. I had nothing. The only thing I knew was I couldn't let him kill her. And so, in one hour, I'd be at St. Ignatius's to put an end to this.

CHAPTER NINETEEN

I used my pocket watch to keep track of the time as I made my way to St. Ignatius's. I couldn't allow Bridget to die for me, so I made sure I was staying within Ian's one hour timeframe. I wanted so desperately to go and find Thomas, but I knew that I couldn't. If I did, he wouldn't let me go save Bridget. And if he came with me, they would kill her. Eventually, I stood in front of the tall, ostentatious building that was St. Ignatius's. No one seemed to bat any eye as I made my way into the hospital; the gates had been wide open. I assumed they were all waiting for my arrival. I found my way to Lucinda's office at the top of St. Ignatius's knowing that both her and Ian were most likely keeping Bridget there, waiting for me to come and save her. I was right outside the door of Lucinda's office though, when I stopped breathing.

Screaming filled my ears. I quickly realized they were the screams of Bridget.

"No one can hear you," Ian said. "So go ahead, keep on screaming. You're in a mental institution for Christ's sake. It's perfectly normal to hear people screaming all the way down the hallways."

Bridget looked up at Ian and said quietly, "Please let me go."

I was standing in the middle of Lucinda's office. Before me was Bridget. She was tied to a chair, tears rolling down her face. Standing before her, waiting impatiently, were Lucinda and Ian.

"Be quiet," Lucinda spat at Bridget. She looked at her wristwatch and then turned to Ian. "Where is she? You said this would lure her in."

"It will," Ian confirmed. "Just give her time."

Lucinda walked her to the large picture window behind her desk and looked out at the city of San Francisco.

"We don't have time," she said while looking out the window. "Her birthday is in one month. The prophecy needs to be fulfilled before then, or it will never come true. Our powers will cease to exist, and we will be forced to continue hiding our true selves from the world."

"She will come," Ian said again. "I promise you."

Lucinda turned on her heel and walked toward Ian, her heels clicking against the floor as she did. She grabbed Ian by the chin and looked directly in his eyes.

"You better hope she does," Lucinda said. "This could have all been over the first time around if you had done your job right."

"I'm not the one who put my trust in a woman who was clearly insane," Ian replied.

Lucinda cackled at that. "Bessie was insane, but she did her job. She went and got herself killed at the hands of Abigail. Which is what we needed. You, on the other hand, could've encouraged the girl to save her fiancé. If you had, we would have only needed her for the last part of the process. Instead, we've been chasing her down here in San Francisco."

Ian didn't respond. He looked away from Lucinda and back at Bridget. She was giving him a pleading look, but it didn't seem to phase him.

"Why are you doing this, Ian?" Bridget asked him.

He knelt down in front of her and reached out his arm to lightly brush her cheek.

"*My sweet Bridget,*" *he said.* "*You've always been so clueless. You should know that I never felt anything for you. And I know what you are. It hasn't been difficult to tell. So don't sit here and act like you felt anything for me either.*"

Bridget shook her head.

"*You don't know anything.*"

"*What are you two blabbering about?*" *Lucinda spat.*

"*Bridget here is a degenerate,*" *Ian said.*

Bridget's entire complexion reddened and she looked down at her lap, attempting to stifle tears that were coming forward.

Lucinda cackled again. Ian smiled and walked away, a smug look on his face.

Suddenly, time seemed to speed up. It was as if the hours were jumping ahead. The room went from being doused in the late evening sun to being shrouded under the darkness of the night.

"*Well,*" *Lucinda said, again standing in front of her picture window,* "*it would seem the girl is not coming. She knows where Bridget is. I've waited long enough; it's time for our second option.*"

"*Second option?*" *Bridget asked.*

In a moment, Lucinda was quickly behind Bridget and took a blade across her throat. She made the worst sound, and then she had blood pouring forth from her. She was dying. I screamed as loud as I could, but I knew better. No one could hear me in this premonition.

"*We'll send the body as a message,*" *Lucinda said.* "*And we'll go from there.*"

I had collapsed just outside the door to Lucinda's office. I stood up and began to process what I had just seen. According to my premonition, Bridget was going to die. If I walked into that office right now, I would change death's course. Bridget might still die, but I would interrupt the Time Line, which from the sounds of it, is exactly what Lucinda wanted to happen. They had been orchestrating the entire thing. I was supposed to kill Bessie. It all made sense now. I remember clearly on the bridge that night, it was almost like Ian was encouraging me to kill Bessie. And it seemed she had been unaware of that part of the plan. I remembered the look on her face. She had looked as if she had been betrayed. Ian had betrayed her.

They must've known tonight I would be sent a premonition. It was a game of chance, but the game had worked in their favor. And now there was not a thing I could do. Tears cascaded down my eyes as I made my way back down the steps. I had to leave. I had to leave Bridget here to die. I had to leave her to die in the most horrible of ways. If I intervened, time would react, and it would destroy everything as we knew it.

I finally made it to the bottom of the stairs and turned the corner. Standing in front of me was Aldridge. I didn't even have time to react before he violently hit me in the face, knocking me backward. I hit my head hard against the concrete of the steps. Blood was pouring from nose. My vision was blurry, but I could see the outline of Aldridge standing over me.

"Foolish girl," he muttered.

Aldridge grabbed me by the shoulders and began pulling me up the stairs, back toward Lucinda's office. Once he got to the top, he pushed open the door. Lucinda and Ian were in conversation together. The conversation I had already heard.

"We don't have time," Lucinda was saying. "Her birthday is in—"

Lucinda stopped speaking, presumably because Aldridge had interrupted them by dragging my body into the room.

"Abigail!" Bridget shouted.

I knew then and there it was done. I should never have come here, but I had.

BOOM.

The entire hospital shook with a violent force, and the glass of the picture window blew out of its frame. Was this time reacting? The entire room started to shake and pictures began to fall from their places on the walls. Books began to slide off shelves. I observed all of this while on the floor, moving my eyes to the directions of the various sounds.

After the shaking stopped, Aldridge spoke up.

"I followed her up here," he said, "and I waited at the bottom of the steps. She was starting to leave, just as you had expected she would."

Aldridge pulled me up and into a standing position. He held my hands tightly behind my back.

Lucinda nodded at me, her hands on her hips.

"Of course, she did," Lucinda said, a smile appearing on her face. "Abigail only wants to do what is right, even if that means her friend has to die."

"Abigail," Bridget said. "Did you have a premonition about this? You shouldn't have come."

"They tricked me," I replied. "I tried to leave, and Bridget, I'm sorry I did."

"It's okay," Bridget said, tears on her face. "I understand."

"So sentimental." Lucinda stood watching us, a look of pure evil on her face. But then her face changed, as if she'd just had a wonderful idea. "I wonder…"

Lucinda walked over to the chair that Bridget was tied to and began to untie her. "Ian, help me."

Ian did as he was asked and soon both Lucinda and Ian had a hold of Bridget. Lucinda began to drag her over to the shattered window.

"Stop it," I shouted. "What are you doing?"

I pushed my body forward, but Aldridge's grip was hard to break. If there was one thing my mother and father had taught me, it was to fight any attacker, not give into them. So I brought my foot up between Aldridge's legs and showed him what I truly thought of him. He yelped in pain and immediately let go of me. I ran forward, just as Lucinda pushed Bridget out the window.

Everything happened in a matter of seconds. Neither Ian nor Lucinda attempted to stop me. Either they were shocked I had gotten away from Aldridge, or they truly didn't care whether Bridget lived or died. I threw my body to the floor at the edge of the window, the shattered glass cutting into my skin and grabbed Bridget's hand. My other hand clasped the curtain that bordered the window. I knew it wouldn't last long.

I was suddenly looking down at the ground below. Lucinda's office was higher than I had thought. Way higher. And Bridget was barely holding onto my hand. Our hands were both sweaty and her hand began to slip from mine.

"Hold on," I said. I attempted to pull the curtain, hoping that it would allow me to pull Bridget up. But it had the opposite effect. The curtain began to tear from its rod.

"You need to let me go, Abby," Bridget said.

"No," I said. "Please, God, no."

"Abby," Bridget said, tears pouring from her eyes. "Look at me."

I looked back at Bridget and for a moment we locked eyes on each other.

"I want you to know," Bridget said, "that I've always *loved* you. And I know you loved me as a friend, but not that way. But that's the reason I've acted the way I have sometimes, and I'm sorry for it. And I still love you."

Bridget let my hand go.

"No," I shouted, letting go of the curtain and watching Bridget falling, falling, falling away from me.

I rolled over on my back to face the ceiling before she hit the ground. I couldn't see that happen to my friend. I couldn't bear it.

Clapping and hideous laughter broke me out of my thoughts.

"That was quite intense," Ian said, continuing to clap and laugh. "Wouldn't you agree Lucinda?"

In that moment, I let hate consume me. It felt like the worst feeling in the world, but I hated Ian Cross. And hate fueled my body as I grabbed a shard of the window pane that lay next to me, pushed myself off the floor of the office, and brought the shard up to Ian's neck, but I hesitated, and stopped. Ian wasn't moving. He was completely still. I looked over to see Lucinda extending her hand toward him; she was using her powers to freeze him in place.

"Do it," she said. "You know you want to. He deceived your best friend. He deceived you. He deserves it."

I hesitated, unsure of what to do. I could try to end this all now and take out Lucinda instead, but she would probably expect that. And on top of that, could I do it? Could I actually kill someone? Sure, I had let go of Bessie. But there had been no choice. She would've done something much worse if I had pulled her back up.

"You've already done it once," Lucinda continued, taunting me. "Kill him. Kill him like you killed Bessie."

I dropped the shard. I couldn't bring myself to do it.

Lucinda withdrew her hand, unleashing Ian from his frozen state.

"Foolish girl," she said to me. She held her hand up and I was immediately frozen in place. She walked forward and touched my cheek.

"Eventually," Lucinda said, "these powers of mine will have no effect on you. I will make you the greatest Timekeeper this world has ever seen. And you will rule alongside your sister. And you will lead us all into a new dawn. A world where Timekeepers will be in charge. A world where we will not hide away and assist the human scum with how to run their governments and what decisions would be best for their country. It will be glorious. Take her downstairs."

Lucinda looked over at Aldridge. He nodded and quickly moved to take me. I was still frozen, unable to do anything with my body except allow others to do what they pleased with it.

"Be quick," Lucinda said. "We won't have much time and we need to get to the American Headquarters so we can use the Time

Line to travel to the London Headquarters. From there, we will finalize our plans. I will be along shortly."

Aldridge carried me in his arms. He led us out the door of Lucinda's office and down the flight of stairs that would then lead to the spiral staircase into the main building. When he reached the main floor, he gave a story to one of the receptionists, saying he was taking me to the basement for testing. She only nodded at him. No questions were asked. However, there was a man at the receptionist's counter asking questions. It was Thomas. He looked over when Aldridge spoke and then looked away, but then quickly looked back again when he realized it was me.

I started to feel a sensation in my fingers. Lucinda's powers were wearing off, as had Bessie's when she had used the same powers on me. It was because I was an original Timekeeper. I suddenly regained all moving ability in my body and didn't hesitate to make a fist and punch Aldridge in the nose. He cried out and dropped me. I hit the floor. It hurt, but I quickly got into a standing position, grabbed Thomas' hand and dragged him along with me.

Together, we ran out of the hospital and toward Thomas' motorbike, parked just outside. We jumped on and I clasped my arms around his waist. He didn't hesitate to put the bike in gear and speed away.

"There isn't time to explain," I said, "but we need to get back to the Headquarters and get everyone out of there. And Lucinda and Aldridge are coming there, so we need to be careful."

"Okay," he said as he navigated through the traffic, "but do you ever follow directions?"

"I'm sorry," I said into him, "but I had to save Bridget."

He didn't ask any more questions. Thomas was smart enough to know that I had failed based on the fact that Bridget wasn't with us.

"How did you know where I was?"

"Alma said you went to look for Bridget," he responded, "and considering how long you were gone, I assumed the worst."

Even though I was crying, I smiled at that. Thomas continued speeding through the streets of San Francisco to the nearest entrance for the San Francisco Headquarters.

CHAPTER TWENTY

The closest entrance to the San Francisco Headquarters was the Ferry Building. Thomas quickly swerved his motorcycle into a spot by the curb in front of the building and we both climbed off. He reached out and I took his hand. He dragged me along with him as we ran into the building. As soon as we walked into the main building, we took a sharp right and headed through a door marked *Maintenance Only*. He took me around a corner and then we went through another door he quickly shut behind him.

As he had done for the entrance through the library, Thomas found a design of a clock on the floor of the room, placed his pocket watch on it, and it began to reveal a hidden staircase. He quickly pocketed his watch and beckoned for me to follow him. As we descended into darkness, the room above quickly closed away as the floor slid back in again, concealing the entrance. We walked in darkness for a moment, lower and lower and lower. Finally, we stepped off the last step and into a narrow passageway. There was one door to the side, but at the end of the passage was the Time Line.

We moved closer to the Time Line and I could tell something wasn't right. From our view point, at the right end of the Time Line, the line was no longer straight. Instead, the Time Line had stopped and a new line was forming directly underneath it.

"My God," Thomas said as we walked up to view the Time Line.

"What's happening to it?" I asked.

"It's as if it's resetting itself somehow."

I looked up at Thomas. "Resetting itself?"

"Yes." The response didn't come from Thomas. I turned and found Elijah standing behind us. A look of utter horror was on his face.

"Elijah," I said. "I need you to tell me everything. I've already messed everything up. Tell us what will happen."

"The world as we know it will cease to exist," Elijah said, in shock. "Time is going to try and reset itself—and the only way to do that is by wiping out humanity. Think of it like an Ice Age. There will be earthquakes, tsunamis, and devastating weather-related catastrophes. It will start here in San Francisco, and then it will continue to spread throughout the world, like a virus, until the weak are wiped out entirely. Only the strongest will survive; many will be Timekeepers as they will use their premonitions of what is to come to survive. This is the prophecy the dark Timekeepers wish to fulfill. They want to bring in this new age with you ruling alongside your sister."

I walked up to Elijah and grabbed him by the lapel of his jacket. We both looked into each other's eyes and then I dragged him over to the Time Line and pointed at the disaster I had created.

"Elijah," I said, "you've always been there to provide me with what I need. I need you to snap out of this and tell me how to fix it, because I am not about to let this woman destroy the world because she wants me to be some kind of ruler. Tell me how to fix this. *Please.*"

"You need to go to the original Headquarters," Elijah said. "It's in —"

Elijah was cut off as he made a terrible, horrible cry of pain. We both looked down to find the blade that had once belonged to Thomas' grandfather, plunging through his stomach and coming out the other side. The blade was quickly pulled out again and I looked up into the eyes of Council Headrick. Elijah dropped to the floor, grabbing my hand as he did. But his death was quick. He looked at me once more, but before he could get out another word, his eyes closed. My uncle was dead.

I looked from him and back to Headrick and then to Thomas and then back to Elijah on the floor. Everyone around me was dying and if people were going to say it wasn't my fault, that I didn't cause this, well I could honestly say I felt they were wrong. In that moment, I wished I was a normal Timekeeper. No. I wished I could just be a normal human being. I didn't ask for any of this. I didn't ask for my mother and father to die. I didn't ask for Phillip to die. I didn't ask for Ian to betray my trust as Bessie had done before him. I never wanted Bridget to die, and now Elijah? It was too much. It was all too much.

"Don't move."

It was Headrick who had spoken. I looked up and saw Thomas trying to inch forward, but she had the blade extended outward, clearly ready to plunge it into him if need be. Headrick, her eyes still trained on Thomas, began to speak to me. "Abigail, you are coming with me. You were clever and managed to outwit that idiot Aldridge, but you won't do the same with me."

"It was you," I said suddenly. "You killed Winston, didn't you? You were there that night. All of the Council members were."

"Of course, it was me," Headrick said. "I've played my cards well. How do you get people to trust you and like you Abigail? You're nice to them. You tell them what they want to hear. Winston may have been a misogynistic piece of work, but he didn't know how to play the game. If he was smart, he would have truly convinced his peers he wanted to make the world, our world, a better place. And right when you have them convinced, right when you have them under your thumb, that's when you pull the rug out from under them. That is when you take over. I know how to play my cards Abigail.

"Now, we are going to wait for your grandmother to arrive and neither of you will move an inch, or I am going to plunge this blade into Jane's chest. Lucinda will be here momentarily, and she will take you with her to London, as was originally planned."

"Why did you have to kill him?" I asked. "He was about to tell us where the original Headquarters was located. Isn't that something you need? Isn't that information you would have wanted?"

I didn't know what else to do. I had to keep her distracted while I figured something out, and I hoped that Thomas was trying to figure something out as well.

"No," Headrick replied. "On the contrary, we don't need the place at all. The prophecy can be fulfilled without even entering the place. And I didn't want you to know the information either. I've heard the rumors—the stories. I don't need you messing anything up for us."

Her words made my brain's wheels spin. Maybe, just maybe, there was a way to correct this mistake at the original Headquarters. Mathias had told me the rumors. He'd said there were stories that the original family could change things—that they had more power than a normal Timekeeper. I needed to get there. I needed to find the Headquarters. But first, I needed to get out of this mess.

Just at that moment, I saw a shadow at the end of the hallway. It was Alma. She had entered almost as discreetly as Headrick and stopped dead in her tracks when she saw the blade pointed at us and Elijah's body on the floor. We had to keep Headrick looking at us. I trusted Alma. She would think of something.

But Headrick was about to turn and see her.

"No," Thomas shouted.

Alma grabbed a decor vase from a stand at the end of the hall and began moving quickly, but quietly.

"Jane," Headrick said, turning back to face him and raising her blade, "I've always respected you as a Timekeeper, but that doesn't mean I won't plunge this blade right through your heart. What is it?"

"I just wanted to say to be careful."

Headrick gave another questioning expression. "Be careful of what?"

"This, bitch."

Alma stood directly behind Headrick and slammed a vase into her head before she even had a moment to respond. The vase smashed and Headrick fell to the floor, dropping the blade.

"Grab her," Thomas said. "Both of you. Now!"

We did as we were told. Thomas turned around, taking out his pocket watch again, and clicking the travel button on it. A projection of the globe appeared and Thomas quickly selected a location. Thomas then placed his pocket watch around Headrick's neck.

"Throw her at the Time Line," he said.

I looked at Alma, she shrugged, and we both threw Headrick's body into the Time Line and there was a bright flash. Her body vanished into thin air.

"That was amazing," I said, "but your pocket watch, it went with her."

Thomas looked at me with a grin on his face. "We can't use them anymore." And then he jumped into action.

"Alma," he said. "I need your help. We need to warn everyone that they need to get out of the city as fast as possible. There are going to be catastrophic events happening. And we need to be quick, because some not-so-great-people are going to be here soon to use the Time Line. I need you to use your pocket watch to send a message, and then you need to get rid of it. If we don't get rid of it, they can use it to track us. Abigail, you'll need to leave yours as well."

"Just the one I received at my initiation, right?"

Thomas shook his head. "You should probably leave both."

"What if we need the one Eleanor left me with?"

Thomas looked annoyed, but then he nodded. "We might. Let's just hope it can't be tracked."

Alma looked back at the Time Line as she took her pocket watch out. "Where did you send her?"

"For a nice trip to Antarctica," Thomas said, the grin returning to his face.

"Won't that just send her to someone else's Headquarters?" I asked.

"Nope," Thomas said. "The Time Line works differently when you are traveling in the present. It will simply drop you into the location that you request. However, you have to be careful, because if there isn't a Time Line in that location, you're stuck coming back the normal way."

"And there isn't a Time Line in Antarctica, is there?" I asked.

"Nope." Thomas grinned again.

In a split second, however, the room began to violently shake. I fell backward and landed on the floor, as did Thomas and Alma. A line split into the ground down the hallway, and rubble broke from the ceiling. It was over within seconds.

"We need to get out of here now," Thomas said. "There will be tsunami's next. I need to call Oliver. He has a plane. It can seat four, but that's it. Are you coming with us Alma? What about your family?"

"My family left for Europe after the ball," Alma replied. "Do you think they'll be safe there? Why can't we travel through the Time Line?"

"There's a lot to explain," Thomas said, "but Elijah said that the catastrophes will spread like a virus, but that it will start here in San Francisco. Your family should be safe, for now at least. As for the Time Line, the Council has been infiltrated and they will be able to track us if we use it to travel. We can't risk it. Alma, send the message now."

"What is she going to do exactly?" I asked.

"I told you, if they are programmed to our Headquarters," Thomas said, "they can be used to send messages."

Alma took out her pocket watch and turned a few dials and then shut it. Within seconds my own pocket watch, not my mothers, but the one I had been given at initiation began to make a loud squealing sound from my pocket. I took it out and opened it.

This is Alma James of the American Headquarters. Everyone needs to evacuate San Francisco now. Get to the Time Line and go to Europe. You need to leave immediately, or you face imminent death. I wish you the best.

"Alright, both of you, leave your pocket watches here," Thomas said. "Let's go. We need to get to the military base on Treasure Island. Oliver is there and he can get us a ride out of here."

Alma and I dropped our pocket watches on the ground and followed Thomas up the stairs that would lead back out the entrance of the Headquarters and into the Ferry Building. As we soon as stepped back onto the streets of San Francisco, another earthquake hit. Cars moved across the streets unwillingly and buildings were swaying. It wasn't as bad as the last one, and thankfully neither had been that bad, so it looked like all buildings were still intact.

"There will be tsunamis soon," said Thomas as he climbed on his bike. "I guarantee it. Both of you get on and hang on tight. I'm going to move fast."

As soon as Alma and I climbed on, I heard shouts. "There she is."

I swung my head around and saw Aldridge. He was pointing at me; Lucinda stood behind him. And then another earthquake shook the city and both of them stumbled.

"There's no time," Lucinda said as Thomas began speeding away. Within moments, the two of them were out of sight as we headed in the direction of Treasure Island.

Thomas drove his bike on the road that was just on the edge of the bay. He led us into the East Cut and then made a U-turn so he could get onto the Oakland Bay Bridge. As he did, another earthquake hit. Everything began to shift. I turned my head and literally saw the streets rising up and down as the quakes spread throughout the city. And then I saw it—the Russ Building. It was the tallest building in the city; it had been for almost twenty years. And the building was starting to come down.

"Thomas," I said.

"What?" he said, clearly irritated as he navigated around the various traffic trying to escape the city.

"The Russ Building is coming down."

"What?" This time his tone was shock.

"She ain't kidding," Alma added in.

"Shit, shit, shit," Thomas said. He pressed harder on the gas and the bike sped up.

"Um," Alma said, "not to burst anyone's bubble, but the Golden Gate Bridge…"

We all turned our attention to the Golden Gate Bridge. The wires holding the bridge up began to snap as it swayed in the bay from the magnitude of the earthquake. And then, in a matter of seconds, the bridge came down into the ocean.

I looked back ahead of us and saw Thomas driving straight for a car in our path.

"Thomas, look out!" I shouted.

He looked ahead again. "Shit!" The bike swerved sharply to avoid hitting the car that was in front of us. Alma and I managed to hold on as Thomas sped up even faster, knowing full well this bridge wasn't going to last as soon as the quakes caught up with it. It was only a matter of seconds before the bridge started swaying.

I looked behind us and saw the bridge coming down on the other end. Cars began to fall into the bay. We didn't have much time before it caught up to us.

"Thomas," I said, looking forward. We were almost there, but not quite as the bridge was beginning to separate from the island.

Thomas didn't slow down, he pressed down hard on the gas and pushed the bike to go at the fastest possible speed.

There was now a large gap between the end of the bridge and Treasure Island.

"Thomas," I said. I didn't know what else to say. I squeezed his waist harder, as did Alma to mine. "Thomas, Thomas, Thomas..."

I put my head against his back and closed my eyes.

"FUCK," Thomas shouted as pulled the bike upward, sending us into the air, off the bridge, and onto the island.

As soon as we were on the island, Thomas stopped the bike and looked back. We all did. The bridge fell away into the water, the cars and people that were on it along with it. Screams. Cries of agony. People shouting, "help" were all I heard as I looked back. All of this destruction. All of this chaos. All of this death. Caused by me.

And then the sirens came on. The sirens from the Coast Guard telling us a tsunami was coming.

"We need to get the fuck off this island," Thomas said. He put the bike into gear and we began racing toward the military base that Oliver was at.

As soon as we got there, Thomas pulled to a screeching halt. Surprisingly, Oliver was there waiting for us. He ran up to Thomas and gave him a hug.

"How'd you know we would come?" I asked.

"Oli and I are all we have on this island," Thomas answered me. "He knows we'd never leave each other and that this is where we would meet."

"But what if something happened to Thomas?" I asked.

"It's Thomas," Oliver replied. "I'm not trying to boost him up and put him on the spot or anything, but as you could probably tell from your adventure on that bike, the man's got talent."

"Well," Thomas replied, "as much as I'd like to stay here and discuss everything that makes me wonderful, I think we need to get off this island. And like right now. Can you get us out of here? Do you have a plane?"

"Everyone's left already," Oliver said. "But, yes, I've got a plane. What kind of question is that? Come on!"

Oliver led us toward the runway where sure enough a civilian plane that would manage to seat us was waiting.

"Abby, hurry!"

I had stopped in my tracks. Instead of keeping up with everyone, I had turned my attention to the city of San Francisco. The skyline was laid out perfectly in front of my eyes and to the right of the city was a tsunami that would devastate it in only moments. This was my doing. I did this. And now I was running away from it.

"We have to go back," I said. "We have to help them."

"There is NO time!" Thomas screamed at me. "If you want to help them, we have to leave and find another way."

"Thomas is right," Alma added. "Abby, you can't fix this here. We need to go!"

My eyes began to water, and I felt hot tears falling down my cheek. I fell to my knees and put my head in my hands.

I felt a hand on my shoulder.

"We need to go, now," Thomas said.

"No," I said, "just leave me. Leave me here. If I die, there's nothing more she can do. It's over."

He pulled me up, but I pushed him away.

"Get off me!"

"Abby," he yelled, "I am not leaving you here."

I was screaming now. My entire body shook and scratched at Thomas' face, but he was persistent. He was not going to leave me here.

"ABBY!"

Thomas grabbed my shoulders and pulled me into his arms. I was beating him to put me down. I was screaming to be let go. He was stronger than me, though. He had me pinned in his arms, keeping me from getting any further away from him.

He grabbed my face in his hands and then he pressed his lips to mine. Pulling away, he looked into my eyes.

"That was REAL," Thomas said. "And I won't leave you here, because if I do, everything will have been for nothing. We can't fix this if I leave you here. And I will never be the same if I lose you. I know how much you've lost, but can you fight for me Abigail? Only you can overcome this darkness. I NEED you to overcome this darkness. You've changed me, and I love you, Abigail. I love you. Now is the time to send this darkness and despair back to wherever the hell it came from. Can you do that?"

In that moment, I remembered my mother, Annette Jordan. She had told me she knew who I was. That I wasn't a bad person, that I would do great things. And in that moment, she lifted me off the ground. I nodded at Thomas and began to run toward the plane with him.

"Let's get out of here!" Thomas shouted as we reached the plane. Oliver was already seated in the pilot's seat and Alma was with him. Thomas and I climbed into the seat behind them and Oliver took no time to start the engine and get us moving. Thomas positioned me on his lap and placed a helmet on my head.

A roaring sound disrupted my racing thoughts, and I saw the wave heading toward the city. It crashed into buildings. The Chambord Building, the home Bridget and I had made, would soon be under water. The water washed over the remains left behind by the devastating earthquake and in turn, would leave the city in shambles.

The tsunami touched the back of the plane as soon as we lifted into the air. The plane rocked down, but Oliver managed to lift it back up and fly away from the tsunami that was tearing San Francisco apart. Thomas and I were tucked together in the back seat. Alma was up front with Oliver. We were getting out of this today. We were going to make it today.

I looked out at the city below. The waves had washed over the city. It was almost entirely covered by water. Treasure Island was being impacted by the tsunami as the plane rose higher and higher into the air. As the plane flew away from the city, my mind was no longer consumed by the darkness. I no longer heard Melanie speaking terrible things in my mind. I had fought against her voice, her influence. Ian would never again take advantage of me and my kindness. He would never again drug me. I had fought against Lucinda's influence. We would meet again, I knew we would.

In that moment, I felt like I had ascended from being a person consumed by everything that had destroyed my life. I was done feeling sorry for myself. I was done being upset about all the terrible things that had happened to me. Instead I was now angry. I was angry at my sister, even though I knew I couldn't blame her entirely for everything. I was angry at Aldridge for manipulating me. I was angry at myself for continuing to allow myself to be manipulated. I was angry at Headrick for misusing people's kindness for her own agenda. Finally, I was angry at Lucinda. At the end of the day, everything led back to her. She was responsible for this as much as I was. She was responsible for me being taken away from Mathias just as I got to know him. An idea she fed to Headrick, no doubt. She was responsible for my mother's death and for my sister's imprisonment and brainwashing. In that moment, I made a vow to end Lucinda. I would fix this. I would fix all of this, or I would die trying.

Acknowledgments

I would like to thank all of my readers that have continued to support me in my writing endeavors. I appreciate my readers giving *The Timekeeper's Daughter* a chance, and then coming back for round two in *Within Darkness*. It truly means a lot.

Thank you to my family: Mom, Dad, Anthony, and John for being supportive in the writing that I do. It means a lot. Thank you to my grandparents, Jack and Leona, for always asking how the book is going and for your input. It is greatly appreciated. Thank you to my aunt Natalie, and my cousin Mary for being my number one fans. Much love to you. And thank you to all others of my family for your continued support.

To my friends, you know who you are, thank you for buying my books and being supportive of my writing. I appreciate your feedback and your wisdom.

Much appreciation to my editor, Andrea Berthot, for painstakingly combing through the book and finding those things that all writers miss, even in their own editing.

Once again, thank you to Alexander von Ness for the beautiful cover design and translating Abigail and her story into a visual.

And finally, thank you to my Grandpa Roger, to whom this book is dedicated, for his support of my first book and always buying copies of it and passing it around the family. I wish you could be here for this one, but I know you are up there with Grandma Paula rooting us all on.

CPSIA information can be obtained
at www.ICGtesting.com
Printed in the USA
BVHW031730300119
539057BV00003B/13/P

9 780578 403205